*Praise for Zach Williams's*

## BEAUTIFUL DAYS

"Like Gabriel García Márquez and Stephen King, Williams understands how unnervingly intense and unknowable children can be. Like J. G. Ballard, he savors postapocalyptic vistas. But Williams is his own writer. . . . He pushes you slowly off into the night, then down long embankments . . . we might be staring before long at [the] *Selected Stories of Zach Williams*."

—Dwight Garner,
*The New York Times Book Review*

"A glorious creepfest . . . Williams sees beyond newspaper headlines to a world cleaved apart by forces we've unleashed, blinkered by arrogance and greed. . . . *Beautiful Days* is the spear tip of his potential. This writer's got talent to burn."          —Hamilton Cain,
*The Washington Post*

"Nothing thrills a book reviewer more than a debut book so electrifying, so original, such an auspicious announcement of a major talent, that it makes the hair stand up on the back of your neck. I am delighted to say that Zach Williams's story collection, *Beautiful Days*, is such a debut."          —*The Boston Globe*

"At least once every year, a debut short-story collection comes along and gets under my skin. . . . In 2024, that collection is *Beautiful Days* . . . a subtle and speculative barn burner that fans of Stephen King and Ling Ma will devour."                           —*Esquire*

"Remarkable. . . . Revelatory. . . . Williams's tales deserve favorable comparison to the stories of Wells Tower and George Saunders."

—*Publishers Weekly* (starred review)

"A brilliant debut."

—Jeffrey Eugenides, Pulitzer Prize winner and author of *The Marriage Plot*

"Zach Williams is a brilliant, singular, deep, and deeply entertaining writer. You will continue to think about and feel these stories long after you have finished reading them. They will change you."

—Jonathan Safran Foer, *New York Times* bestselling author of *Here I Am*

"*Beautiful Days* is a remarkable collection . . . full of surprises and truths and stuff we never imagined."

—Percival Everett, Booker Prize finalist and author of *James*

"*Beautiful Days* brings a reader through strange and grounded lands on just the other side of reality. You will come through changed, shaken, thoughtful, and totally amazed."                    —Samantha Hunt,
author of *The Unwritten Book*

"[Zach Williams's] beautiful, disquieting stories are profound in the true meaning of that word—they go deep."                    —Hari Kunzru, author of
*White Tears*, *Red Pill*, and *Blue Ruin*

"*Beautiful Days* contains elegant mysteries, and the book stays in the mind long after you've read it."
—Charles Baxter,
author of *The Sun Collective*

"The visionary weirdness of these stories feels hauntingly attuned to our time."
—Elizabeth Tallent, author of
*Scratched: A Memoir of Perfectionism*

"Wide-eyed on the world and its often mystical ways, there's a sparkle of magic and mystery in every elegant sentence of these wondrously curious, unsettling, and absolutely original stories."
—Chang-rae Lee, author of *My Year Abroad*

"[A] bracing debut. . . . Lyrical, well-crafted, offbeat yarns."                    —*Kirkus Reviews*

ZACH WILLIAMS

# BEAUTIFUL DAYS

Zach Williams is a Jones Lecturer in Fiction at Stanford University, where he previously held a Wallace Stegner Fellowship. His work has appeared in *The New Yorker*, *The Paris Review*, and *McSweeney's*. His story "Trial Run" was one of three that won *The Paris Review* a 2023 ASME Award for Fiction. Originally from Wilmington, Delaware, he currently resides with his family in San Francisco.

# BEAUTIFUL DAYS

# BEAUTIFUL DAYS STORIES

## ZACH WILLIAMS

VINTAGE BOOKS

A DIVISION OF PENGUIN RANDOM HOUSE LLC

NEW YORK

Published by Vintage Books, a division of Penguin Random House LLC, 1745 Broadway, New York, NY 10019. Originally published in hardcover in the United States by Doubleday, a division of Penguin Random House LLC, New York, in 2024.

Vintage and colophon are registered trademarks of Penguin Random House LLC.

Several pieces originally appeared in the following publications: "Neighbors" and "Wood Sorrel House" in *The New Yorker*, "Trial Run" in *The Paris Review*, and "The New Toe" in *McSweeney's Quarterly Concern*.

The Library of Congress has cataloged the Doubleday edition as follows:
Names: Williams, Zach, (Zachary Conner), [date] author.
Title: Beautiful days : stories / Zach Williams.
Description: First edition. | New York : Doubleday, 2024.
Identifiers: LCCN 2023043061 (print) | LCCN 2023043062 (ebook)
Subjects: LCGFT: Short stories.
Classification: LCC PS3623.I566647 B43 2024 (print) |
    LCC PS3623.I566647 (ebook)
LC record available at https://lccn.loc.gov/2023043061
LC ebook record available at https://lccn.loc.gov/2023043062

**Vintage Books Trade Paperback ISBN: 978-0-593-68574-7**
**eBook ISBN: 978-0-385-55015-4**

*Book design by Casey Hampton*

penguinrandomhouse.com | vintagebooks.com

Printed in the United States of America
10   9   8   7   6   5   4   3   2   1

The authorized representative in the EU for product safety and compliance is Penguin Random House Ireland, Morrison Chambers, 32 Nassau Street, Dublin D02 YH68, Ireland, https://eu-contact.penguin.ie.

*For Rosalie*

# CONTENTS

# BEAUTIFUL DAYS

# TRIAL RUN

pitched through the lobby door, and then, as I caught my breath, stood looking back at the storm. It was bad out there. The city had been reduced to dim outlines and floating lights; snow moved down Nineteenth Street in waves. I beat it from my hat and coat, knocked my boots together. Under those high ceilings, each sound reverberated. Only the emergency lights were on, there was no one at the front desk, all the elevators in the bank sat open and waiting. And in a fit of hope, I thought there might not be, in all the building, even one other soul.

The elevator stopped on nine, though I hadn't hit that button—silence, nothing but cubicles in the faint light of an alarm panel. When the doors slid open again on fourteen, I saw Manny Mintauro, our security guard, like a stone slab behind his podium. Half his face was in shadow. My heart fell at the sight of him.

"Sup, bro," he said, deep and grave.

The elevator doors closed behind me. "Hey, Manny." Snow dropped from my jeans onto the carpet. "Thought it might just be me today."

"Nah."

Manny's head was pristinely shaved, and his gray scalp, textured with follicles and curled across the bottom with fat, gave the impression of a thing horribly exposed. It called to mind a dream I've had: Pulling fistfuls of hair from my head, I discover that what's beneath is the yellow-white pith of an orange. In a rising panic, I claw at it.

"Well," I said, "I guess it'll be pretty dead, anyhow."

"Definitely. Weather's crazy." He gave *weather* two hard syllables.

It was hard to know when you were done talking with Manny. I was still getting used to having him around, watching all our comings and goings. Since the mass shooting at Rantr the previous spring, it had become common for tenants of downtown buildings to staff in-house security. Manny had served in the Marines during the Gulf War. I often wondered if, there at the podium, he was armed, or how exactly he was authorized to use force in a security situation. That was management's phrase: security situation. During the monthly lockdown drills they'd instituted, Manny paced the emptied corridors, testing the handles on the conference-room doors, unblinking, while we crouched inside.

I said, "Power's out at my place, so I'd rather be here. All things considered."

"I'm obligated to be here," Manny said. "Hey, just so you know. There's another TruthFlex email. Came in just now. Delete that shit." He covered his mouth with his hand. "Pardon my language."

"Ah. Damn. Another one. Sorry—sorry to hear about that."

"You don't got to say sorry to me, bro. You know what I mean?"

I didn't. And anyway, that was enough, the encounter was sufficient. I drew a breath, pulled up my shoulders. "Well—have a good one, Manny." Hoping he'd yield, I moved toward his left flank.

Instead, his head reared back. "Real quick, before you go—I've been meaning to say to you." His tiny eyes held fast to mine. "When, the other day, I told you about the most important moment in history, in my opinion? I realized that I didn't ask what you thought was the most important moment in history. To you."

The week prior, Manny had cornered me in the men's room and talked at length about the Balfour Declaration. I hadn't understood his point, but he'd leaned against the door, and I'd felt trapped.

"Huh," I said. "I'm not sure, Manny."

"To me, the Balfour Treaty is the most important. Did you look it up?"

"Not yet. I've been pretty swamped."

"It had a big impact on global history."

"I do think I learned about it in school."

"Nah," he said, "you can't learn nothing about it in school. You know what I mean?"

"It's one of those things you know you've heard of."

"You have to do your own research. Look into the Rothschilds. Follow the money."

"Okay. I will."

"Nice." He appraised me carefully. "Let me know. I'm curious how you think, is all." Then he dropped his left foot and angled away, opening a channel where I might pass. He extended his right hand, leaving the pinkie and ring fingers curled tightly into his palm, and grinned down at me as I took it.

It was dark on the fourteenth floor, all the monitors black and cold. One other person had come in, though. Shel Bunting. He sat craned over his computer in the corner by the window. I might have been glad to have him there—to help with Manny. But something had always seemed the matter with Shel. In meetings, he hardly ever looked up; he just focused on the table. His face was pale in some spots, blotchy red in others—on his forehead, or under one eye, or across his throat. No one really knew him, but I sensed a hidden reserve of strangeness in Shel; I'd always felt he needed looking at, and as I crossed the floor, I stared into my phone to preempt any possibility of eye contact.

I dropped my bag, put my coat on the chair, sat and swiveled so neither Manny nor Shel was in my line of sight, and took out my laptop, running my fingers along the deformed place where the battery had swollen. A note from Lisa, our manager, still sat near the top of my inbox—"Stay warm, see you back at the office on Thursday." But just above it was the one Manny had mentioned, from TruthFlex00-09@gmail.com: "Lisa Horowitz is a CULTURAL MARXIST—¡WHITE GENOCIDE!"

For six weeks now we'd been receiving the emails and still no one knew who sent them. It was a mystery. We weren't supposed to open anything from TruthFlex, but I couldn't help it; I always clicked. If TruthFlex posed a threat to me, I wanted to understand it. We all knew someone who knew someone at Rantr. Anyway, the emails were largely indecipherable—weird screeds in shifting fonts. Sometimes there were YouTube links: "White Pride Is Healthy and Moral" and "100 Fake Hate Crimes Staged by DemocRAT Leftists." Nearly all the emails targeted Lisa by name, and the first had arrived just after she'd signed us up for mandatory diversity workshops, so of course we wondered if TruthFlex might be one of us. But as far as we knew there weren't even any Republicans in the office, much less far-right fringe types. It was a small analytics firm, everyone was well educated, and at thirty-eight I was one of the oldest employees in my department. Anyway, the police had said TruthFlex might well be no one in particular, someone who'd burbled up from the deep for reasons obscure, or else a bot, even—it happened all the time, evidently. The IT people blocked each new Truth-Flex address; that didn't matter. They couldn't prevent us from receiving emails. And the police said there wasn't much they could do until TruthFlex made an actual threat. Besides, management reminded us, we had Manny to keep us safe. Before the first lockdown drill, we were told to brainstorm all the objects within reach that might stop a bullet. I kept coming back to the windows—if I could get out to the other side of them somehow . . .

Somewhere behind me, Shel sneezed. I looked at my phone. It wasn't even ten o'clock.

I decided to text Bradt: *Lmk if power comes back?* But he rarely woke before one. Bradt was a Craigslist roommate, still in his twenties; he'd moved in after my divorce. I tried never to text him—each new message exhumed the preceding, laying bare the bleak business of our lives together. Today's stood beside one from December 19: *Hey man im sorry but thats too loud.* Bradt made a living as a video-game streamer. Tens of thousands of kids, apparently, tuned in to his channel. I'd never watched, though sometimes I googled him; he generated a good deal of commentary in some minor culture war, the semantics of which were obscure to me. Though everything now felt obscure. If the years between Bradt and me seemed unbridgeable, what would the generation behind his be? It was hard to imagine they'd still be human—I pictured something like a waving blue bed of sea anemones. Bradt worked from a two-monitored desktop computer in his room, clad in gym shorts and headset, and spent weekends out of town. No idea where. Sometimes I'd wake at night and hear him in the hall, muttering to himself. I didn't know what anchored him to the outside world, and in those moments, transfixed, I'd half dream Bradt opening the door, light spilling in, the boundary between us collapsed. So I couldn't go home. Bradt was there, offline and untethered.

Coffee would mean walking past Shel to the kitchenette, so instead I looked at Facebook: a video of Louis C.K. talking about gun laws, strangers fighting in the comments. But the seventh batch wouldn't load, the wheel spun into perpetuity, and as I watched it, I understood I couldn't reasonably avoid Shel all morning. If I just made chitchat with him on the way to the kitchenette, I'd be done: both Manny and Shel accounted for.

I closed the laptop, stood, pushed in my chair.

As I moved across the floor I watched Shel, anxiously, and Manny watched me.

"Morning, Shel." I leaned over the top of his cubicle, smiling.

"Hey there." He was unshaven, in a lumpy black sweater. Below his desk was a gym bag, packed tight, heavy looking. Shel didn't seem like he exercised much. He was thin and soft.

"Just us, huh?"

His splotches glowed. "And Manny."

"Manny," I said, glancing across the floor at his podium—he looked up from his phone and met my eyes. "What a character."

"Manny?" Shel asked. "How so?"

"Oh, I don't know. You ever talk to him about history?"

"No."

He waited, I supposed, for me to go on. I felt I'd said too much. A sudden gust battered the window; snow stuck to it in patches, and we both turned to look.

"I should've stayed on Long Island," Shel said. "But I couldn't sleep, I came in early. Before it got bad."

"There you go. That's the way." I smiled, and he did, too. Was that enough? Yes: We'd agreed on exactly one banality. I'd be justified in ending it. I coughed, then said, "Well, Shel, I'll let you get back to it."

"Sure." He folded his hands on the desk, looked down at them. "See you."

"Have a good one." I rapped the top of the cubicle partition with my knuckles and stepped out, free.

But somehow, as I walked, I could feel him behind me, pulling, slowing my steps. It was like I knew I could walk forever and never reach the coffee machine.

And then Shel arced his voice over the length of floor I'd put between us: "Hey, actually—can I talk to you a second?"

I turned back. He sat facing me, hands on his knees, eyes hidden in the dull glare off his lenses. Slowly I retraced my steps until I was back in position before him, all progress lost.

"Sure, Shel. What's up?"

He sighed, then laughed; I noticed a tremor in his leg. "I hope this isn't weird, but, I don't know—maybe it's stupid, I'm sorry if it is—it's just, since there's no one around, and since you walked over and we were talking, I thought I might say to you—well—I know you and your wife split up." He coughed into his fist. "I'm sorry to bring up something personal like that, but I wanted to because, because, that's something we have in common. Now, I mean. You and me." He smiled weakly.

"Oh, God, Shel," I said, miming sympathy with a hand on my heart. "I'm so sorry. I'm so sorry to hear that." And I saw I'd been defeated. He'd insinuated me into his life. Countless trips to the kitchenette, hundreds of elevator rides, so much would be spoiled by this.

"Thanks." Then he let out a long breath; his whole body relaxed. "You're the first person here I've told. I keep to myself, you know, but—you've always been a nice guy. And then there you were. And this day's so weird."

"Well, you know, you're young," I said. "You're—how old are you?"

"Forty-one."

"See? Young enough to start over. I'm—you know, my divorce was—it gets easier."

He reddened. "Yeah. Well. I bet your ex didn't try to fuck you over as bad as what mine's doing. Or I hope she didn't." Abruptly he said, "Can I talk to you in earnest? In confidence?"

"Shel," I said, "of course."

He crossed his arms and looked out the windows. "I'm in pretty bad trouble. She spent months conspiring with this piece of shit attorney."

"Okay," I said. "I'm sorry to hear that."

"He got her to record me with her phone. In secret. During big fights."

"Okay."

"She'd goad me, you know—push me, willfully, to get me to say things, certain things, that sound bad, but anyone might say them, under the circumstances." He shot his eyes at me. "Did you and your ex have big fights?"

"Well—sometimes. Not—I don't know. Big fights?" I looked over my shoulder. Manny watched from the podium.

"Apparently she has me—according to this oily, disgusting lawyer, you know—they have me on the phone telling her . . ." He sighed, his face flushed. "Telling her 'I'll fucking kill you.' And other stuff like that. Bad stuff. Worse. I'm such an idiot."

Shel's desk was right up against the plate-glass window, but the snow was falling so hard now you couldn't see much of anything, except where it blew past the streetlights. They were on because of the storm, and the city had put in new LED bulbs that shone a cold, harsh white, like over a stadium, or a prison yard.

"But she'd needle me and torture me."

"Right—I mean, Jesus, Shel."

"And now they'll use it to keep me from my son. When the truth is anybody might say those things, if you were put in the position I was put in, in terms of the mental torture she employed. A deliberate campaign against my—my sanity, basically. And this lawyer has a team of operatives who follow me into stores. They monitor my Internet use. It's an illegal campaign."

"Okay."

He appraised me carefully. "Between you and me, I wonder about Manny. They hired him right around when all this stuff got bad. I was nervous about being here with him alone. But I had no choice. See, I can't go back to the house. I'm between spots right now, and actually—I stayed here last night. I slept under my desk."

We both, in that moment, turned our eyes toward the patch of carpet at his feet: a power cable held together with electrical tape, one unbent paper clip.

I said, "Oh, Shel."

"I'm sorry I lied before."

"That's okay."

"About coming in from Long Island."

"That's okay, Shel."

His face contorted. "Anyway, I figured Manny wouldn't be in. Now I'm wondering if they sent him because they saw I didn't swipe out last night. Did he say anything to you? What were you two talking about earlier?"

"Nothing—I don't know."

"He wasn't talking about me?"

"Shel, no, of course not."

"History, you said? Whose history? Like browsing?"

"The Balfour Declaration," I said. "Manny likes the Balfour Declaration."

He eyed me. "They think I'm TruthFlex. Did he say that?"

"No, Shel. Jesus—no."

"Because I sent Lisa an email telling her I'm not going to those fucking diversity workshops anymore, I refuse. This PC shit is out of fucking control. So now they've got the cops interviewing me about TruthFlex. Did Manny tell you that?"

"Shel, no. I'd tell you. I wouldn't keep it from you."

And then it was like a spell had broken. A puzzled look crossed his face; he removed his glasses, let them hang from his hand as he pushed his palm into his eye. "God. I shouldn't have done this."

"It's okay," I said.

"You've heard more from me than you ever wanted to. It was too much."

"No. That isn't true."

"Well. I bet it is."

"No, it isn't. In fact," I said, deliberately, "I'm happy to talk. Anytime."

He put the glasses on the desk, sat back, looked out the window. "You know something? I can't tell you how much that means to me."

I took a step closer, laid my hand on his shoulder; I squeezed, and his sweater bunched into the folds of my palm. "Thank you," he said. His computer went to sleep, the screen shut off. "It means a lot," he said. "You taking a minute to talk. I'm not kidding. I haven't had many people to talk to." He put his hand on top of mine. "You're a good guy."

. . .

In the handicapped stall I sat on the toilet with the lid down and looked at my phone. The system had suddenly blown off course, defying the models; the snow was heading out to sea at an almost unbelievable pace, and we would be spared the brunt of it. An incredibly unlikely scenario, but there it was. Meteorologists defended themselves hysterically on Twitter. People on Facebook seemed enraged that the storm wouldn't hit harder; they jeered at the mayor. Three feet had been the prediction, but the recalibrated models now said five inches, almost all of which had fallen already. The storm was just going to vanish.

I'd have to report Shel. There was no question about that. He was unstable, possibly delusional, an abuser, evidently, and he lacked the basic judgment not to reveal those things to a colleague. Anyway, he might well be TruthFlex. Who else, if not him? Shel needed help, that was clear, and I hoped he'd get it. But what if there were guns in that gym bag? I'd tell Lisa. Though I guessed I could go to Manny. Was this the sort of thing he was there for? Did Shel constitute a security situation? I imagined the blank look Manny would wear as I fumbled through my account of the conversation, stopping to append important details I'd omitted. No, I'd wait for Lisa. It would have to be face-to-face; I didn't want anything in writing. In the meantime, I'd grab my things and slip out. I'd need to make it past Manny, which wouldn't be easy. But I'd take a day alone with Bradt over this. For a moment, though, I did nothing at all—it was nice there, cocooned in the stall, fourteen floors up.

Everything was brighter as I walked back to my desk. The snow had stopped, all but some flurries, and the sun was coming out. Down through the windows, I saw plows pushing snow off the street. I began to pack, quick as I could. Then I glanced up. Manny was moving toward me.

His voice rang across the floor like a shot: "Sup, bro."

"Hey, Manny," I said, nodding at the windows. "No more snow."

He squinted. "Something weird about that, right? A few hours ago, they were so sure this was the big one."

"So, I think I'm going to head home."

"All good," he said, leaning over my cubicle. There was a smell on him, some tonic, sharp and chemical. "I wish I could go home."

"Maybe if Shel leaves?" I ventured, wondering if he'd understand. "Is it—do you have to stay—because of Shel?"

He frowned. "What's up, bro?"

"I'm just a little worried about Shel."

"Nah," he said, looking down at me. "Shel's cool."

"He's had sort of a tough stretch, sounds like." I searched Manny's face for signs of comprehension. "I was talking to him before," I said, hoping that would clarify things. "What I'm saying is I think he might need some support. I care about him. You know?"

"You and Shel? You two are the only ones who're

nice to me. Everyone else here is rude as fuck, excuse my language."

"I only wanted to mention it."

"No problem." Peering around Manny I saw that Shel, in the distance, was reclined in his chair, arms crossed, watching us. "It's just that," I said, growing desperate, "we were talking about TruthFlex."

"TruthFlex." Manny shook his head. "That's all noise, bro."

"What do you mean? There's no threat? Do you know who TruthFlex is?"

"Isn't it you?" He laughed, jabbed me with a fat finger.

"Me?" I recoiled, hands up.

"Relax, bro. I'm fucking with you."

"It isn't me. I'm not TruthFlex."

"Right, I know. 'Cause *I'm* TruthFlex."

"You are?"

He shifted his weight, adopted an open posture. "You want me to tell you? My money's on Lisa."

"*Lisa?*"

"Lisa's not any kind of typical bitch." He covered his mouth. "Pardon me. But you know what I'm saying? She knows how shit gets done. Listen, you can't talk honest like this to everyone—you have to know who to trust. But we're cool." He shook my hand again, fingers in the same crooked arrangement. "You have to educate yourself," he said, still tightly holding on to my hand. "To me, the most important event in modern history, in terms of where we are right now? Is the Balfour Treaty."

"Right." I tried to pull my hand back; he wouldn't let me.

"Look, bro. The Ashkenazi Jews are extremely intelligent and capable."

I bit my cheek. "Of course."

"And they went through one of the worst atrocities in history. You see pictures of those concentration camps on the Internet. All those people all fucked up." With his free hand, he covered his mouth. "Excuse me."

"No problem." He let my hand go.

"And yet it became an opportunity. In terms of the Ashkenazi Jews then spread around the globe. They were refugees. The nations of the world took them in. And now? They run this shit. You see what I'm saying?" On any other day Manny would have been called away long ago, back to his podium to hand out a visitor badge, or I'd have been carried off in the usual traffic around the floor. "In a certain way of thinking," he went on, "it's like, you take a loss to make a gain. Sometimes that's how business is done. You follow what I'm saying?" He unbuttoned his jacket and leaned on the top of the cubicle partition, very close, directly between the exit and me.

"I think so," I said, understanding now that this had always been Manny, the real Manny, just like that, back there, was the real Shel, hiding below the surface of routine, awaiting, with all the patience of a fanatic, some dark eventuality in which to reveal himself. They were members of a strange league, known to each other by instinct, traded glances, preparing for something in secret, perhaps not even the same thing, but the same in tenor and spirit. And they had identified me as one among them.

"Lisa's sending that shit herself, bro. Making out like she's getting fucked with. See what I'm saying? She's taking one from her team's playbook. Next thing you know she'll get a promotion. You watch." He shrugged. "It's all good. Like I say: Me? I keep my head low. But I know something's going on. Shit's funny right now." He nodded toward the windows. "It's almost go time out there. Think about it. The only reason I got this job is because they're shooting up schools and shit. Something's coming, bro. I don't know what it is. I just watch. I wait. You understand? I know how to take care of myself. When it happens, I'm good. You see me? But all these people"—he looked in the direction of the empty cubicles—"they think shit's going to be like this forever."

An idea broke over me: I could call a car. I wasn't powerless. I opened the app, found I'd gotten logged out, got the password wrong twice. "I don't mean to be rude, Manny," I said, looking down, "I just need to—"

"And I'm thinking: What do they really want me here for? Who wants me here? You know what I'm saying? I got my eye on them, too. The management, and whoever's in charge of them, and whoever's in charge of *them*. I try to spot them when they slip up—or when they want you to think they slipped up. Like this storm. How's a storm like this just going to disappear?"

"Yeah." A car was on its way, blinking down Park Avenue. In horror I watched Shel, across the floor and in shadow, stand, push in his chair, and begin to move toward us.

"Look. At the end of the day, the reptilians pull the strings. Hillary Clinton fucked up and shape-shifted into her reptile form when she was on *Kimmel,* bro. I'll send you a link. I'll send you links to all this shit. It's all on YouTube. Let me get your home email."

My phone buzzed. TruthFlex00-02@gmail.com: "RAC-IST Lisa Horowitz Hates White People."

"TruthFlex," I whispered.

He laughed. "See? Lisa's sending that shit, eating fuckin' breakfast in bed."

Shel was fifteen paces out now, walking with his hands in his pockets. The three of us were converging into a singularity. And that was impossible—the building couldn't sustain it. Together Manny and Shel might have enough power to make it real, whatever it was they wanted.

But then the notification flashed on my phone. I thrust it out for him to see: "Manny—I'm sorry. My car is downstairs."

He took a step back, inhaled sharply through his nose. I kept the phone raised, a talisman to ward him off.

Flatly, he said, "All good, bro."

"I called a car. It's here now." I waved the phone in Shel's direction; he peered at me in the dark.

Manny stared down. "I took up too much of your time."

"Not at all," I replied, keeping one eye on Shel, returning the phone to my pocket, hefting my bag. "I'm sorry to have to run."

He winked. "To be continued," he said, reaching out with those two bent fingers again—the shape of a gun, it now occurred to me.

I shook Manny's hand. And when I got to the elevator bank, I took the stairs.

On the street, the sun glared off the new snow. I had to squint and shield my eyes, but the city was recognizable again. If the storm had been what Manny suggested—a hoax or an experiment, a drill, a trial run—it was over now, the data collected, people everywhere resuming peacetime postures. A black sedan sat at the curb with its flashers on. The driver craned to look at me through the window; I turned my screen toward him to prove my identity.

As we pulled into the flow of traffic, I closed my eyes and tried not to think of Manny and Shel, still on the fourteenth floor, together now in the dark. Maybe by tomorrow it would all be forgotten. But it wouldn't. I saw myself, in another universe so near to this one as to be overlaid, there with them still, the three of us standing wordless beside the podium, a triangle, arrested in that final configuration. I'd have to report Shel. And Manny. Both. I wished it were automated—done already, somehow, by some watcher or arbiter, absolving me from the fringes. And maybe then the watcher would report me. I just wanted it over with. If I knew how to find the watcher, I would confess everything, whatever it wanted to know.

I'd confess that I, too, hated the diversity workshops;

I hated Leigh Randi, the pleading and humorless facilitator, who sat cross-legged atop the table and spoke to us in a sort of Internet slang. I'd confess that sometimes I turned down the brightness on my phone to take surreptitious photos of women on the train. And that I'd masturbated to images of my ex-wife's sister on Facebook. That I'd lied to Shel—we had had big fights, my ex and me. That we'd fought so loudly outside a bar that a man had sprinted across the street to ask if she needed help. That, once, I'd knocked her to the floor—an accident, I was horrified—pushing with my shoulder against the bathroom door as she tried to hold it shut. I'd confess that I'd lost most of my friends in the divorce. That fantasizing about shooting myself helped me fall asleep. I pressed my head against the cold glass. Sooner or later, everybody was going to find me out.

Bilal, the driver, spoke about Mecca and Medina, the holy cities. A sacred light shines from them, he said. It's visible from space; astronauts have studied it, but they won't reveal what they know for fear of mass hysteria. Still, the important facts are online, piecemeal, for anyone who knows where to look. He laughed often, high and owlish, and asked if I believed in God. I told him yes. I would have told him anything, and the river sparkled in the sun below the Manhattan Bridge.

"Hello?" I called, entering the apartment. The power was still out; my voice echoed in the cold.

"Bradt?" No answer. But in the sink I saw a cereal bowl, brimming with water and milk.

Absently, I tried to lower my bag onto an end table that was no longer there. There were still shadows on the hardwood where the old furniture had been. Then, from the back of the house, I heard something. A low roar. Cautiously, I walked toward it.

There in the deep, away from the windows, it got so dark that I had to keep one hand on the wall. As I neared the hall's crook, where it turned right toward Bradt's room, the sound grew louder. My fingers, searching, found the doorway to my room—what was my room now, the smaller, windowless one, where I'd once thought a baby might sleep. Weakly, I called Bradt's name again.

Then I turned the corner.

Bradt's door was shut, but from underneath and along the sides spilled blue light and terrible sounds: gunfire, explosions. Bradt cackled and jeered over it, his tone vulgar, words indistinct. And it was just like a dream I've had—what I mean is, it was a dream I've had. The dream and that moment were the same: watching the light, listening, flipping the switch on the wall up and down, up and down, up and down, to no effect.

# WOOD SORREL HOUSE

1

It was a modest summer rental, the kind Ronna recalled from girlhood trips to Maine or Vermont or the Finger Lakes, set in a small clearing on a thickly wooded mountainside, peacefully out of sight of roads or neighbors or anything else. Jacob opened all the doors, came back downstairs, and remarked a little sternly that the cottage needed updates: the range wobbled, the mattress caved in the middle, the woolly plaid sofas were from another era. Still, there was something idyllic about the place.

They unpacked into daisy-papered drawers and put their toothbrushes behind the spotted mirror. Max got his very own room. When he woke crying in the night, Ronna walked down the hall and took him from the crib—

a wooden antique with rattling bars. On the shelves in the den, molted antlers served as bookends. A *Hi and Lois* strip hung in a frame there. "I've been coming to this old cottage since I was a little girl," it read. "I love the smell of mothballs, the beat-up furniture . . . the rickety porch . . . There's no TV, telephone, or Internet! But that is what I like best!"

That week, a hot front rolled up the mountain. They spent an afternoon in the forest by the stream. Wiry insects skated on eddies near the banks; woodpeckers sounded overhead. Ronna repeated the word, to teach it to Max: "Woodpecker." He could say more and more and was newly walking. When he tripped over a root, she stood him up and brushed away the pine needles. In his fire-truck shirt and blue summer shoes, he set off again, dragging Quinn, his cloth doll, by the leg.

Climbing back to the house, they saw the snapping turtle for the first time. The light had deepened, but the day was still hot, teeming with flies and gnats. The turtle stopped to watch them from the grass beside the path. It was enormous. Pale mud streaked its shell; its skin was gnarled. It might be a hundred years old, Ronna thought. They did live to ages like that—staggering, cartoonish ages.

Max turned his shoulders, pouting. "Too scary," he said.

It was his one conceptual word. What he meant by it was hard to say. The turtle was scary, but so were spinach and nap time.

Jacob said, "No. It's pretty. Look." He set Max down, squatted behind the turtle, curled his fingers under the shell on either side, and lifted it into the air.

The turtle splayed its legs, twisted its neck, showed its tongue and teeth as if gasping.

It must have nested nearby.

The next time she saw it was weeks later, or months, if months was the right word. In those early years, or whatever they were, she grew strangely attached to the turtle.

Nights, once Max was down, Ronna and Jacob would play Risk—an old set, the box's split corners held with masking tape—and talk their way along the edges of the hard questions. For example, their car: Where was it? There wasn't even a driveway. Had someone dropped them off? From whom had they rented the cottage? For how long? How much time had passed before these questions occurred to them? How much more before the questions grew urgent?

Jacob argued that the way to understand the situation was through numbers, facts, records—anything they could observe and set down, because that was the way you solved a puzzle. But Ronna felt sure that the place didn't follow those rules. She tried to show him what she meant. For instance, his plan to track the moon's progress in his journal. It was, of course, a good idea. If the moon did behave oddly here, that might suggest further lines of inquiry, a chain of discoveries. But think of all the nights when he'd realized with a start that the moon was already up, that he'd forgotten the project altogether for who knew how long. He'd pull out all the drawers in search of the spiral notepad, which most of the time he couldn't find, despite looking behind the bookcase and in the cellar and below the kitchen sink and under the sofa, where once, on his belly, an arm extended, he caught his fingers in a mousetrap. On the handful of nights when he did find the notepad, he'd run down the porch steps into the moonlight. He'd stay out for a long time. Then he'd come back all glum and drop it, still open to his earnest sketches, onto the floor.

"And," she added, "a handful of nights—what if that's not right? What if it's dozens? Hundreds?"

"Don't exaggerate," Jacob muttered, lying on the rug, eyes hidden in the crook of his arm. "It isn't hundreds."

They were supposed to draw a line on the floral wallpaper for each new day. But they'd fight over who'd done it, or whether it'd been done twice. A small and impenetrable forest of ballpoint ink had sprung up there. Jacob's beard grew into his mouth, his hair ran past his shoulders. Ronna would push it out of his eyes and offer to cut it, saying he looked uncomfortable. He'd tell her that comfort was a distraction; they had to stay focused. Her own hair she cut with the heavy scissors from the kitchen drawer— old-fashioned, black-handled, like the ones she remembered from school. She'd stand in front of the bathroom mirror, a towel around her shoulders. Max's hair somehow didn't seem to need cutting. In fact, it hadn't grown an inch. And his fingernails—could Jacob remember the last time they'd clipped Max's nails?

"No," he said. "I don't know. Cut them, then, if they're long."

And he went back down the steps to the cellar. He'd been obsessed by the chest freezer there: When and how and by whom was the food replenished? He was determined to sit unblinking in front of it until he got some answer. "But," he admitted one night, amassing his forces, blue, to threaten hers, green, in Siam, "I don't think— somehow it doesn't . . ." His voice broke, his eyes welled. "I think maybe it isn't allowed."

She crawled over the board and put her head on his shoulder.

It was always summer on the mountain. Mornings, when Max's crying woke her, Ronna would see how well he'd done by the hue of the light on the pines. She'd walk down the hall—softly past the spare room, which Jacob, with his insomnia, now used—and find Max waiting for her, holding the crib's bars. She'd pick him up, kiss the top of his head, smell his hair, take the pacifier from his mouth, and drop it into the jar on the dresser. "*Quinn-n-n*," he'd sing as she carried him back to her bed. Every night, they placed the doll on her nightstand, a little ceremony they had together: *Good night, Quinn, good night, Quinn. I'll see you in the mo-or-ning.* It was the only way he could bear to part with the thing; if she let him take it into the crib, he'd play with it for hours and never sleep. So, at sunrise, reunited, Max would pull Quinn tightly to his body, then push the doll away to appraise it. Ronna spoke for Quinn, chirpily: "Good morning, Max." "Morning," he repeated. The doll's head slumped to one side. "Did you have a good night's sleep?" She watched the trees moving. Cool air bled through the screen. All the mornings fanned out together, like reflections in facing mirrors. Max, looking at Quinn, would nod and say, "Good sleep."

For Jacob, the final memory was a pale-white morning, sun in his eyes, and a downtown bus approaching. He thought he was coming from the gym. For Ronna, it was scrubbing Max's back in their old blue tub. Around those moments Jacob nursed little mythologies: Maybe he'd missed a sign flashing in the sunlight that morning, or there'd been some code meant for Ronna in the galaxy of bubbles on Max's skin. On the floor of the den, legs crossed, eyes closed, Jacob would lead guided meditations: walking slowly down flight after flight of imaginary stairs, focused on breath, hands and feet tingling, trying to wrench the memories loose and uncover behind them something new, no matter how trivial, so long as it lay beyond the horizon of the sun in his eyes. Or the soap. But he worried. What if, under scrutiny, their memories grew unstable, eroding or degrading with the addition of confabulated parts? The final bridge to their old lives might crumble. What if the memory practice made things worse? About this problem he could speculate endlessly. Occasionally, it terrified him. He'd run his hands over his head, staring into the distance as he spoke, and Ronna would listen, feeding Max peas, or bouncing him on her shoulders, or lying with him and Quinn on the carpet, playing trucks.

Giving up the memory practice, Jacob moved on to enumeration, listing, between turns at Risk, each reliable aspect of their new lives, no matter how trivial, hoping to piece together some rough cosmogony of the place. "Here," he'd begin, "there is day." Ronna—it was a stupid exercise, she hated it—would reply, "And night." Sun, moon, grass, trees, blue beetles, occasional rain, ferns that withdrew at the touch of a finger, the sign in the yard— WOOD SORREL HOUSE—and, beyond that, the porch steps and the porch itself, the hall table and the high staircase, the cellar steps and all the dust-covered things at the bottom of them: the fishing pole and the wading coat, the crutches with the torn yellow padding, a tool chest, a sledgehammer, a gray tarp, a pile of red bricks, and a toy bucket and shovel that Max liked to use in the green plastic sandbox out back—Little Tikes brand, in the shape of a turtle.

"What about the snapping turtle?" Ronna offered once.

The night was lush; moths battered the screens.

Jacob collected six blue armies. "The snapping turtle?"

"Yeah." The last time she'd seen it was one morning, near dawn, just after Max had begun to cry in his crib. No light yet on the pines. The turtle had lumbered over the grass, leaving a trail through the dew. "It's the only one of its kind we've encountered. It's particular, among the wildlife here. The birds and grasshoppers are indistinct.

We often hear them without seeing them. They might be a kind of set design, a flourish. But the snapping turtle—it's got some kind of . . . I don't know how to put it. Stature. Doesn't it? Or character. It feels realer to me."

She rolled the dice.

"Say more." His tone was keen; she'd pleased him.

She thought of the time she'd seen it with Max in the birch grove. "Scary," he'd whined again. But the turtle had watched them pass—really watched. "You can see a mind behind the eyes. It's so old. Older than us. It's been here longer; its experience of this place must run deeper. Too much experience. Decades. It's almost cruel: What does it do here with so much time? I don't know. I've got questions about the snapping turtle. When I see it, I feel . . ."

"A sense of something larger. You're right. A wider world."

She nodded, drew a breath to continue, then stopped. It was a delicate subject with Jacob—the one aspect of the place he wouldn't talk about. Max would slip and fall on the rocks or in the woods, and she'd race to him, turn him over, hoping to find his skin broken. It never was. Her skin had bronzed and cracked, new wrinkles ran from her eyes. But Max was the same. He never had learned *woodpecker*. In the notepad, she'd written down everything Max could say: *Mama, Dada, Quinn, hat, outside, uh-oh, dirt, play, nose, waffles*. She hadn't let herself work from memory, she'd waited until she heard each word anew. *Light, bath, nap, scary*. Soon, she'd stopped needing to update the list.

"Maybe," she said, "Max will live as long as the turtle."

Jacob was silent. If she didn't look up at him, she'd be able to keep talking. She stared into the Risk board's blue compass rose. "Or longer. I don't know how to think about it. I'm trying. Maybe he'll be here when the house collapses, and the forest dies, and the sun goes dark." Her eyes were unfocused, her throat was dry. "Isn't that an incredible thought?"

"The snapping turtle," Jacob muttered. "You're right. Where does it go?"

There were rows of old paperbacks on the shelves, spines laced with faults. They didn't appeal, but she'd read and reread them all: *Gone with the Wind* and *The Pelican Brief* and *A Case of Need*. One day, Jacob thought to look up *wood sorrel* in the dog-eared Peterson guide. Then he went out, found it growing all through the clearing and into the trees. It looked like clover: three heart-shaped leaflets, joined at the stalk. Ronna watched Jacob crane over the book, gray and haggard, a bunch of wood sorrel in his hand, and she thought suddenly of his vigils in the cellar, when they were still new here—his vow to solve the riddle of the chicken thighs and mixed berries in the freezer.

He snapped the book shut and said, "It's edible, Ron. You can cook and eat this stuff."

Much later, long after he'd left for good, she'd lie out for hours in the wood sorrel, half dreaming that the lawn was absorbing her gently. One afternoon, she looked up the hill toward the house—run through with summer light, its doors and windows flung wide—to see Max crawling backward down the staircase inside. She was achy and spare, her sunburned scalp showed. He shouldn't do that, she thought, sitting up and shielding her eyes. But when, halfway down, he pushed off the stairs to stand, she laughed: a little mountain climber. There was even a comic aspect to the way he fell, straight back, arms wide, as in an old cartoon. The sound of his head hitting each step carried down the hill. When she opened her eyes, he'd come to rest on his back, stone still, by the hall table. What if maybe he's dead, she thought, standing to cross the lawn. An unhurried breeze stirred the tops of the pines. By the time she'd reached the porch he was halfway up the stairs again, on hands and knees. She sat down in the doorway, drifted off, and woke up in the dark.

## 2

The first time Jacob went exploring, he returned with rabbit skins, ragged and patched with gore, hanging from his bag. "I figure I'll get better at it," he apologized, letting them fall to the porch. That night Ronna bathed and put Max to bed by herself—Jacob was too exhausted—and then they talked on the couch in the den, he with his head across her lap. "I found a lake," he said. "You follow the stream down the mountains to where it levels, then on a little ways, and then it opens up, all at once, onto the water. I saw the sun glinting on the surface through the trees and thought I was dreaming, or dead. The water's cold and clear. There are fish in it."

She whispered, "Fish?" It was somehow astounding.

Jacob said he wanted to find the edge, if there was one. If it turned out that Wood Sorrel House was in the real world, then the edge would be a road, or a town—it would be the edge of their seclusion. If, instead, the place was something constructed, the edge might be more literal. Such a discovery would be horrifying. But then, at least, he would be able to map the interior. "I wonder," he said, "if it's automatically generated, somehow. Maybe it's creating itself as I go. Like, I could walk for the rest of my life and it'd just be different configurations of the same trees, the same hills." But maybe not. Maybe if he walked far enough, he'd find a change in the pattern. "Imagine if there were cities. They might be strange to us; the people in them might not be people, exactly." There might be anything out there. Enough to fill lifetimes.

Ronna ran her fingers through his hair. "I tried to stick Max with a sewing needle today. I wanted to see if I could hurt him. You know?" Feeling her voice shake, she bit her cheek. "I was scared, because what if I could? But I told myself that the way to take care of him, sometimes, is by hurting him. Like an inoculation." Bent over his crib, she'd held the needle above the soft underside of his forearm. "But I kept dropping it," she said. "I couldn't do it. And I didn't know if it was me, or him, or the place. I really wanted to do it. I kept trying."

Jacob lay with his eyes closed. "I climbed the high mountain."

"Yeah?" She wiped her cheeks with her shirtsleeve.

"I got above the tree line. I could see in every direction."

She waited.

"Nothing but trees. I could see the lake. I could see other mountains. A chain. But it's wilderness, it's all wilderness. Miles and miles. No roads. Nothing."

"Could you see us?" she asked. Her mind ran over the day: Max atop her shoulders, leaning to pull a birch leaf from its stem, his outstretched arm before her.

Jacob opened his eyes. "Who's accountable for this?"

Absently, she pressed her thumb to his lips. He kissed it and she pressed again, wanting him to open his mouth for her; she ran her left hand down his chest to his belt and began to pull at the buckle.

He seized her wrist and flung it away.


There was no alcohol in the house. There was, in the medicine cabinet, ibuprofen and antihistamines. She wondered if she could find something psychoactive in the woods. Or poisonous. Though, if she wanted to die, there were better ways. Ceiling beams and rope. Kitchen knives. She could slam her head against the wall, even. Or drown herself in Jacob's lake. His trips out grew longer. She'd stay in bed, a pillow wrapped around her head to dampen the sound of Max's crying. She'd sweat and shiver, talking to herself. But, sooner or later, she'd have to get up. Wash her face, drink from the faucet, brush her teeth. Walk down the hall, turn the knob, open the door. He'd be there, in the crib, diaper sodden, hair matted, eyes dark. She'd stand on the threshold. He'd grab the bars, pull himself up, raise both arms toward her.

Once, Jacob stomped up the porch into the house and pulled Max from his high chair. A storm was coming; he wanted him to see it. Jacob was gaunt and sullen, his beard tied in two long braids. A weird green light fell over the clearing, black clouds crossed the sky. Max squeezed the air between his fingers and whispered, "Too scary." And later, after they'd been without Jacob for a long time, it all happened again: same stony clouds, same cold rain. "Too scary." She wished she could cut his head open and look inside. Had he retained any memory of the first time? Did Max hold on to scary things, or did they pass through him, the way the rain passed over the mountain? Once the blue sky had returned, the storm seemed impossible.

When she asked Max if he remembered his father, he'd only point to something he recognized—a cup, a toy, a tree—and name it.

On his final return to Wood Sorrel House, Jacob carried the snapping turtle impaled on a spear.

Ronna stood on the porch holding Max. "You killed it," she called, horrified.

He smirked. "Nasty fucker tried to bite me."

The spear—the serrated hunting knife he'd found in the cellar, lashed to a broomstick—had sliced straight through the turtle's shell and out its padded chest. Upside down, legs splayed and tail limp, it shuddered each time the spear's butt struck the earth. Max watched as Jacob hung the turtle with rope from a tree branch below the house and cleaned it. He worked efficiently. Its eyes were milky, its tongue swollen and foamed with spittle. The ancient skin fell in scraps; the meat was nearly purple. When Jacob was finished, the emptied shell swayed in the breeze.

It had a spine, Ronna thought in awe.

Fried in butter, the meat was gristly and ripe.

"Go on," Jacob urged. His teeth were filthy.

Ronna took a bite. She chewed until her throat contracted and saliva pooled. Then she spat into a napkin.

Jacob slapped the table with both hands. "Max," he said, loud and grinning, "this country life does not agree with your poor old mother."

3

The lake was just as Jacob had described it. Glimpsing it through the trees, she wondered for a giddy instant if it held something stranger than water. But then she skirted it, moving under branches and through heavy brush, until she found a rocky outcropping that spread down to the edge. It was perfect. She'd left before dawn, and now the midday sun baked the rock. She stretched out and fell asleep. No dreams. When she woke, she removed her clothes and stepped into the water. It was frigid. But afloat on her back, drifting out, she felt good. Near sunset, she took from her backpack a can of tuna, a sleeve of crackers, an apple, and a chocolate bar. She ate, then went into the woods to gather branches and leaves and needles; she built a fire on the flat rock and spent the evening feeding it. She told herself scattered stories, watching the sparks on the water.

She stayed nine days. Near dawn on the tenth, she crashed up through the woods in a panic. It was still dark in the trees. She fell, rolled, struck a rock. She couldn't breathe; she thought she'd broken a rib. Even as the sky brightened, the space before her was hard to parse— colors and shapes in the darkness, the woods all the same. She'd have to go back to the lake and start again. But she couldn't find the lake. The sun rose higher, she was thirsty, she wondered if this was what had happened to Jacob. Then she saw the water through the trees. She traced her way back to the outcropping, where the embers of the fire still smoldered, and then out the way she knew she'd come, and when she found the stream she followed it up the mountain.

Max sat in the corner of his crib. The room was humid and dim. Everything he'd had—pacifiers, blanket, the green water cup—he'd thrown onto the floor. Except Quinn. He held the doll close. It was mangled and wet; he must have been gnawing at it. His breathing was slow.

"Max," she said. Then she shouted it, grabbing his shoulders.

He said, "Too scary."

. . .

Well—how *had* it been for the snapping turtle? It had slept in the high grass. In hot weather, it had sat in the stream; it had made its crooked way back and forth across the mountain. The turtle could not think. Presumably, it had barely been aware. But it had lived so long. And what sorts of understanding might be gained in fifty thoughtless years? Or eighty, or a hundred? Couldn't the turtle have gathered some intelligence beyond itself? An intelligence in parallel, or in secret: a remote space, if not in its brain then somewhere else, a hidden compartment in which to hold the character of its experience—bright nights and dark ones, soaking rains, the taste of chewed grass. What kinds of awareness might the turtle have accumulated in a hundred and fifty years? What if it could have lived for a thousand? How long before it couldn't rightly be called a turtle?

Her clothes hung loose, then fell apart; the words in the paperbacks grew blurrier until she could read them only if she bent close, with the shade off the lamp. New light bulbs were always in the closet by the stairs. Bars of soap, too, and extra sheets, talcum powder, needles, and thread. She'd mended Quinn so many times that it wasn't really Quinn anymore—the doll's face had worn away, its clothes were gone. The only things that changed in her life were dreams, so she paid more and more attention to them; she came to feel that all the dreams she'd ever had were connected, as if part of one vast landscape, and with practice she could traverse it, discovering dreams she'd never remembered before. I could drop him into the lake, she thought one morning, as she saw by the light on the pines that he'd woken too early. But suppose he climbed out? I could try to do to him what Jacob did to the turtle. Eyes, tongue, brain, and bones, all scattered. But I can't, she thought. I can't. I can't. He sat, holding Quinn, a pacifier in his mouth, in the crib. She fell down beside it, reached through the bars, put her hand on his head. "Hi, Max," she said. She was shaking, covered in sweat. "Did you have a good sleep?" Max took the pacifier from his mouth and said, "Sleep."

4

Something flew up the stairs toward her, struck her hands as she guarded her face—a blue jay had flown in through the open door. She twisted and fell down the steps, then lay whimpering by the long hall table. Her ankle burned and was discolored; it wouldn't take any weight. She crawled into the den, pulled herself onto the couch, and shivered under the quilt, listening to the bird flit against the rafters.

Upstairs, Max woke from his nap and began to cry.

In the morning, she lowered herself down the cellar steps, seated, her left leg outstretched. The crutches stood in the corner. And then she found the backpack, filled it with food, took a lighter and a knife and the wading coat from its hook. The steps were too steep to climb, so she went out the storm doors into the clearing. She stood looking up at Max's window. Clouds stung her eyes.

She rested that day and the next by the stream, and then she set off down the mountain, on one crutch, in little hops, her left hand tacky from saplings and branches. At the lake she slept through a run of days, sun on her face, and at night she watched fish break the water's surface. Mornings, when it was cool, she gathered stones from the shoreline, piling the flattest and heaviest into cairns. How deep was the lake? Was it possible she'd sink past the edge into some other world? Yes, that was possible. There was just no help for it—any of it. It wasn't as if she could leave him a note. Or one last meal to eat. Or teach him to dress himself or use the toilet. The problem was too big. She had no power over it.

She unbuilt the cairns, stone by stone, pushing each one into the pockets of the wading coat.

But more days passed, and slowly her mind started to change.

Because here's what she could have done: She could have taken him out of the crib. As things stood, it was only if the legs rotted and it crashed to the floor, or the house burned down or blew over or fell apart, that he'd ever be free from it. A hundred years, a thousand. Longer, she didn't know. However this thing worked.

She went into the brush for more wood. Night came and she stared into the fire.

For the sake of argument: Say she went back. She'd take him out of the crib and put him on the floor. Then what?

She'd have to turn and run; he'd try to follow. Impossible. She couldn't. And in the crib, at least, he'd be safe.

But from what?

She threw twigs into the flames.

Well—safe from scary things. Because, left alone, Max would fall down the stairs again. He might tumble down the mountain, crash through branches and over rocks. One scary thing after another, on and on, into infinity. A kind of hell. What if somehow he followed her into the lake, and a current swept him to the bottom and pinned him against her as she rotted? It was possible, she had to concede that. In the crib, nothing would happen. Nothing at all. And that could be holy, in a way. He'd be like a monk, almost. A sort of saint, enshrined, enthroned. Inhabiting eternity.

She surprised herself by crashing into the water, not in some solemn moment, after a speech or a prayer, but on impulse. Exhilarated by the cold, she kicked until her toes hit nothing, the stones pulling her, water throbbing in her ears. There was a hum or a hiss she could hear only once she'd gone under, an aquatic vibration, and then a shock at realizing that this was going to work. But she must have fought, despite herself. It was hard to remember. She found herself back on the outcropping, belly down, legs still in the water.

All the way home to the cottage she felt calm and strange, separated from things by a layer of noise. Max lay asleep in the crib. She kissed his brow; he stirred to life. She rocked him, seated on the edge of the toilet, as a hot bath ran. She washed him clean while he sang to Quinn, and his wet skin glowed. He asked her to give Quinn a kiss. She did it. Then she touched Max's nose, held his body, felt it swell with breath. She fell into the tub and dug at him with her fingers, pressed her face into his neck, gasping to take in the smell of his head.

## 5

She fixed him to her back in a swaddle of cut bedsheets and wore the backpack on her front. Quinn she stuffed down beside him. The straps chafed, and Max squirmed and kicked, sometimes he cried, but mostly, as they traveled, he spoke softly to the doll.

In the afternoon, they passed the lake. A victory. Of course, there was only more forest, all the same. She built a fire beneath an overhanging rock; she ate jerky and apologized to Max for not feeding him. He pouted but then wandered off, picking up sticks and digging with them in the earth. The sun set. They sang to Quinn: *I'll see you in the mo-or-ning*.

In the night, she woke and felt Max breathing against her.

They followed the sun, so she called it west. Sometimes the hills they climbed would level and drop limply back down; other times, they'd break through the tree line to bare rocky stretches, where eagles skimmed overhead. They traveled along a mountain ridge, two beautiful days, but had to double back when they came to a high chasm:

no way down. That afternoon, they saw black bears, three of them, nosing along the mountainside. She shifted Max so he could see and said, "Bears." She stewed and ate nettles; she kicked mushrooms from tree trunks and roasted them. When Max put both hands into the fire, she panicked and started to shout, then stopped and let him.

The trees thinned. No more big pines, only firs, growing shorter and sparser until—it happened so gradually she barely noticed—they were out of the forest. The soil turned sandy and pale. Before them was nothing. Nothing whatsoever. Now and then, she'd look back: the forest's edge, like a wall, and the mountains looming over it, clouds and sky above the peaks, all together like something in a fishbowl. She walked until it was only a green-blue smear, and then nothing. And then they were nowhere.

On her back, Max was quiet and still. The sand was soft and felt nice on her feet. It faded to a dirty white, like smudged paper, and so did the horizon. When the lack of perspective made her dizzy, she walked with her eyes shut. They had no fires. She ran out of water. Sometimes Max whispered things in her ear. Then the last trace of gray was gone from the sand. It was fine and synthetic feeling; when displaced, it whirled in the air with unnatural lightness. The sky darkened, and the air grew thinner; it tasted like plastic. Then the only light was behind her, as if she were walking into a cave. And soon they were in total darkness.

Okay, she thought. What now.

She sat down, slipped the backpack's straps over her arms, and found the lighter. Briefly, it lit the space around them. She pulled Max from her back, curled up with him, and fell asleep.

When she woke, he was gone.

She felt for the lighter and couldn't find it; the darkness jumped before her eyes. But then she calmed herself: He couldn't have gone far. She angled her head to listen, in one direction, then another, and on hands and knees she found the place where the sand went smooth again. In rigid, deliberate movements she crawled out, feeling with her fingers, counting each motion away from the backpack, and then returning. Wider each time, a spiral. Finally she felt a divot in the sand ahead of her, and then another. She followed the indentations out, slow and careful, the blood loud in her ears. Her fingertips found Max's cloth diaper, and then his back, his shoulders, the nape of his neck; she went into a crouch and drew her arms around him. Only later did it terrify her: He'd been sitting perfectly still, staring into the dark.

Back out in the light, it was the first thing she noticed: "Max. Where is Quinn?"

She dug through the pack.

"Quinn," he said.

She looked toward the dark, then at him, and fell into wild sobs.

### 6

First, she knocked out the walls with the sledgehammer from the cellar. Then she dismantled the rooms upstairs from the inside out, chopped up the plaid sofas, the crib, the bookshelves, and the staircase, board by board. No more stairs—only ramps, built from repurposed wood. The house was transformed into something like a dais, with a wide, flat surface.

She doesn't feed him. She leaves him for days in the woods. She has a cage on a rope, like a crab trap; she leads him to the lake and submerges him inside it.

"Too scary," he says, once he's coughed up all the water.

One day, she imagines, she'll unlatch the top and pull him out, cold water pouring from the bottom, and he'll say nothing at all. He'll be quiet and strong. He'll have kept something from before. She believes this not only because she has to but because he's started talking about Quinn. He looks out over the treetops and tells her Quinn is in the dark. In his head must be a picture of the scene, a story he tells himself. And so it stands to reason that he may in some way remember what he's been taught. Maybe he'll remember her. There's a place in the yard where she buries her teeth when they fall out: six little funerals, so far. She brings him to watch. Maybe she'll feel it coming and know to slink away. But, even if she dies there on the ground, the time before she's gone to soil will be, to him, like nothing.

She'll eat less and less, lie on her mat, boil wood sorrel with salt. He'll walk up the ramps, sleep in the grass, play in the bleached old turtle shell. The sun will rise early and set late. There will be beautiful days.

# RED LIGHT

She sat down beside me and said, "I always start by saying that Jane's not my real name, because this isn't real life, and you don't need to know it."

Her face hadn't been visible in the profile pics, so I was thrilled now to find it covered in freckles, hundreds, and I loved her hair, which was wild and springy and smelled sweet, I noticed, as she situated herself on the barstool. She was stouter than she'd made herself look, posing in the mirror, and that was excellent, too, because I love the human body, all of it—its wet messes and sour parts—and there's no limit, or not much of one, to the kinds of bodies I love.

"Okay," I said. "My name really is Parker, though."

"Fine. Buy me a drink, Parker."

I smiled down at the bartender. Jane asked for a double

mezcal, neat—an in-character order, I thought, calculated to match her blunt speech. And that was fine, too. I've learned from my clients at the gym: If you just let people be who they want to be, they'll yearn to repay the favor.

She nodded at my seltzer. "You don't drink?"

"Not much."

"Because you're, like, a fitness guy?"

"Yeah," I said. "I guess. I'll drink from time to time."

"Are you hung, Parker?" She took a big gulp of mezcal.

"Yes." I held her eyes.

"And you can fuck?"

"I can fuck."

"Have you done this before?"

"What do you mean?"

"Fucked in front of someone else."

She was referring to the conditions set in her profile. If I have a type, in terms of profiles, it's ones, like Jane's, that assertively detail a plan, seeking an actor to help realize it.

"A few times," I said, which was only a slight stretch of the truth. Because it's been a lot more than a few. I'm not shy. It's what I love. We're like-minded, my friends and I. It's a good thing.

"I like your muscles, Parker," Jane said, and touched my arm.

I told her I liked everything about her. I told her she was beautiful.

She leaned in, whispered, "I want to taste your cock," and I was fine with that; I felt so good about the energy between us, and my ability to accommodate that specific want of hers, and others as they might arise. We were reaching that familiar understanding, a spiritual one, temporary but very real, where all our needs, no matter how unspeakable in the light of our average days, could be shared—where we could commune deeply with each other, and also with her boyfriend, who, as I had been given to understand, would be involved in his own chosen way.

She moved her hand up my thigh. "Finish your seltzer."

I followed Jane to a walk-up on the avenue between a Mexican restaurant and a florist. She hurried ahead; I ambled behind, hands in my pockets. The night air was balmy. The magnolias were in bloom. She unlocked the door to the building and held it open, waiting for me, her face lit hard by the streetlight. It was awkward, that light, like seeing each other in X-ray, and you can't abide awkwardness in those moments or else the thing you're chasing might disappear. Jane knew this, so she hustled me past the broken mailboxes and up the stairs.

"I'm not turning on the lights," she said, stepping into the apartment. "You don't need to see anything. Walk straight to the bedroom. I'll meet you. And take off your shoes, please."

She vanished into the dark. I slipped out of my loafers and left them in the hallway beside some galoshes and an umbrella. "Shut the door," I heard her call from off to my right, and when I did I couldn't see anything; I came unmoored. My eyes adjusted, and then there was a faint red glow from a doorway down the hall to my left. I followed it, one hand on the wall.

I've seen a lot of these bedrooms. Le Chat Noir and Audrey Hepburn posters. On the bed, far too many pillows and an old teddy bear. Twin Ikea dressers, silver and gold spilling from the jewelry boxes atop them. The scent of lotions. All the photo frames had been laid flat, in preparation, I guessed, for my arrival. I lifted one: family, beach, golden hour. Another: college-era, girls in a pack, close-shot, cheek to cheek in sparkling gowns. Everything was blurred and red—the effect of the silk scarf thrown over the bedside lamp, the room's only light.

Behind me, the door clicked shut.

There was Jane, now decked out in a little cowgirl outfit, totally adorable, with Daisy Dukes and even twin six-shooters, glowering across the room like she dared me to say anything. I grinned, made a low sound in my throat. Between that outfit and the red light and the decor she had revealed herself to me; I felt I understood her; I wanted to show her that she could trust me with all of herself, her most decadent wants, yes, but also her plainness. Whether she stayed in character or came out, my role was to support her.

I felt myself getting hard.

She opened a drawer on the nightstand and took out a silver vape pen. "Do you want some?" she asked, back turned to me.

I put my hand on the freckled skin just under the cute

bow that secured her sheriff's vest; I kissed her neck. She took a drag off the pen and then dropped it, whirled around and thrust her tongue into my mouth, pulling violently at my belt.

"Wait," I said. "What about your boyfriend?"

"I told you. He watches."

"Yeah. Where is he?"

She held my gaze. "He watches from the closet."

"Oh." I looked over her head, around the room. "Which one?"

"Which do you think?" she sneered, whipping my belt off and through the air like a snake.

Only one of the closet doors, I saw, had slats.

"He doesn't want to come out? I don't mind."

"No." She dropped to the carpet, taking my jeans and boxers down with her in one light, balletic motion.

"He could play with us, if you want," I said, tousling her hair, looking at the slatted door. "I could play with him, too." It's not that I like to be pushy—I only wanted to offer them a chance at the things they might not ask for, as well as the things they would.

But Jane had this all worked out already. She flicked her tongue at me and said in a half shout directed at the closet, "Look what I brought home for us, baby."

There was no reply.

We proceeded in the soft red light.

I kept one eye on the closet door, though the room was so dim my vision blurred. Was that movement, between the slats? A cautious finger? The poor guy—too hung up to come have fun. That is, of course, if there really was some-one in there. But I trusted Jane because she was showing herself to me, her real self. When you're fucking the way we were, you can't hide anything. That's the authentic you, incapable of artifice, completely exposed, vulnerable, and therefore full of power, switched-on, humming. It's realer than you'll ever get with most people, even ones you love dearly—parents, siblings, hung-up friends. I know plenty of long-married couples who can't connect the way Jane and I did in that one hour. And once you've shared that with someone, it's theirs to keep. I carry Jane's deepest most beautiful ways of being with me, always, and she carries mine, and no one can revoke or rescind that. And we pass that sacred light down through the ages, person-to-person, because we've been fucking that way for all of history—the Egyptians, Shakespeare, Jesus, all of us—and a thousand years from now, or five thousand, or ten thousand, they'll be fucking that way, too, just like Jane and me, or at least I hope they will, because it's the holiest kind of communion.

And I tried to put on a show for the boyfriend because I wanted to commune with him, too. I waved my body energy at the closet; I pulled out of Jane, scowled, wagged my tongue at him; I flexed my biceps. Each time she came I nodded toward the door, and although I couldn't see the guy, I started to feel a back-and-forth between us, me and him, whoever he was. It sounds funny, maybe, but in that heightened state, I could feel vibrations coming from the closet, through me, and out into Jane. It was gorgeous and so pure.

When Jane was good and ready, I asked where she wanted me to finish. I did it. Then, panting, I fell onto the bed.

When I opened my eyes, Jane was fussing with a box of tissues, holding a cowgirl boot under her arm. "I'm going to the bathroom. Don't move," she muttered and was out the door.

And all at once it was so quiet. I felt my pulse in my head; I let out a sigh. Then I looked at the closet. "Hey, man," I said, "that was fucking rad." I sat up, put my hands on my knees. "You've got a really great girl. You're lucky, man. I love the openness. Did you have fun?"

The door to the hall hung wide, and I understood then that it was a railroad apartment—the bathroom was way on the other side of the building. She would be a minute. I'd hear her footsteps.

"Would you mind if I came and said hi?" I stood up. Slowly I moved toward the closet. "I really loved that. I just want to connect with you before I go. Is that okay?" I laid my fingers lightly across the slats. Then I licked them. And in that moment, his silence didn't strike me as the same as no reply. Words were only one tool for negotiating. I knew it was okay, so I reached for the knob.

When something happens very quickly, you might spend a disproportionate amount of time thinking it over, afterward—much more than you spent experiencing the thing in the first place. And then your memory can grow a kind of skin over that moment. Eventually the skin and the thing it covers are inseparable. Possibly there's more skin than anything else. The memory behaves more like a dream. And that's how this is for me.

But this is what happened. In the closet, there was this little guy. He couldn't have been more than a couple of feet tall. I didn't know if he was sitting up on a shelf or if he had something like a high chair in there. He was just sort of back in the clothes. His head was long and thin with a coarse tuft of orange hair, and the rest of him was squat and stumpy. He had an unusual texture. His skin looked stiff but moist. I didn't see a mouth or a nose, but I heard him respiring—a wet click at the top of each breath. He was just a small, funny thing. A little guy. But he had the loveliest eyes, blue and human, searching back and forth across my face.

When I heard Jane's footsteps, I knew he meant for me to close the door. So I did.

Jane entered, pulling tight the belt on a silk robe. "Do you need anything before you go?"

"Maybe just a bit of that pen."

"It's on the nightstand." She made a show of busying herself around the room as I dressed and took a few drags.

"I had a lot of fun with you both," I said. "Can I give you a kiss good night?"

"Just go, please. The door will lock behind you. I'd prefer if you didn't use the bathroom."

As I worked my shoes on by the apartment door, faint

murmurs bounced from the bedroom and down the hall. They sounded like coos and words of love.

Back on the street, I was so high from Jane's pen. I decided to walk home. It was still early, not quite ten, and my first client at the gym wasn't until noon the next day. Those flowering magnolias gave the air texture and taste, and the streetlights looked green, and so did the windows of the corner bodega, like we were all underwater. I put my hands over my head, felt the night between my fingers. A wave of joy shot up my spine. My whole body sang. Everything was so good.

## LUCCA CASTLE

### 1

Friday morning, Bea walked into the kitchen, dropped her backpack onto the chair opposite mine, and said, "You look like shit." Then she set her eyes on her phone. It was still dark, not yet seven, but I'd been there a long while, staring into a mug of hot water and honey, hearing vague, invented sounds, like distant fireworks. My fever was down some; now I was cold and perspiring.

She asked how I felt. I covered my throat with my hand, mouthed *my voice*, and winced.

"So," she muttered, "no work again."

I supposed I was frightening her.

Bea was fourteen, a freshman, and standing there in her plaid kilt she looked so cold already. Out in the air her legs would prickle, as if plucked, and on each of the three escalators she'd ride up from the tunnels to Lexington Avenue, men would see her, quicken their steps to get behind her, crowd close to smell her, or else, farther back, crane to see up her skirt, and her fingers would curl over its pleated bottom, holding it tight to her thighs, to thwart them. The first time I saw her make the gesture, I thought, she's getting out from under me; she's learning how to be in the world.

"I've got Dr. Harper after basketball," she said, pulling on her down coat, taking up the backpack again. "I'll text you. But I'm running, I'll be late. Don't walk me." I frowned, shook my head, lifted my jacket from the chairback. "Dad," she said, exasperated, "you'll only make yourself sicker," and I knew she was right. But I think that's what I wanted. It was hard to explain, even to myself, but all that year I'd been nagged by the sense that my problem was more than just grief. That my grief was an arrow pointing toward some place I'd have to go.

Nora—Bea's mother, my wife—had been dead a little more than one year. She had died suddenly and by chance, in what I suppose you'd call an accident, just walking to the train from work. The shock of dislocation that I experienced after it happened had been nearly physical, like passing into a new and different city—the streets roiling and unsteady, the buildings overhead a dark mess of stalagmites. Eventually the sensation receded, though I couldn't forget it, and it kept coming back, each time a little stronger. I had to learn to blink it away. For months that's what I did, but it came to feel hopeless. The sensation seemed to want to go toward some extremity, a point of complete saturation. What I grew to suspect was that, sooner or later, I'd have to let it.

On Monday, when I found I couldn't get out of bed, I wrote my father-in-law, Len. For fifteen years I'd been a partner at the private equity firm he'd founded. I told him I was unwell and didn't know when I'd be back at the office. I shut my work phone and laptop in the gardening chest on the roof, and then, in isolation, I gave up health and healthful thoughts. I got rid of every platitude anyone had ever offered, everything I'd been fed in therapy, any notion that Bea and I would be all right again. Whatever chose to come to my head I allowed. I would think of it like an experiment: If I let this thing have its way, what would happen? Maybe I'd come unstuck. This nervous anticipation began to build. I was only lying in bed, but I felt as if I were way out on some kind of ledge. And just as fields of color rise from the dark if you stare long enough, I began to sense in solitude new directions to wander. New constellations overhead.

Then on Wednesday I came down with the fever. Who knows where I'd picked it up—I was no stranger to the potent bugs that travel the city on subway poles and dollar bills. But as I paced the house, waiting for Bea to come home, I couldn't help but imagine that I'd somehow invited the illness onto myself. Just for fun, I decided not to take anything for it. And now, look, it was Friday, and my voice was gone. I wouldn't have said it aloud, would barely let myself think it, but it felt like confirmation, a further step in a process, some necessary calibration or alignment between inward and outward. Necessary for what, I wasn't sure. But that didn't matter. I was sick and miserable and a little radiant. The experiment was working.

## 2

I walked Bea up the block to the avenue. The morning's quick pulse made me anxious—cigarettes smoked in doorways, black coffee and Advil in tear-away packets, buses, whalelike and obscene, swallowing people at one end, expelling them at the other, and at that hour, schoolchildren in packs, the older ones mesmerized by their phones or else braying and pushing, stepping into traffic and back, beating their chests. Bea herself was still so bluntly childish. Just to see her walk, the locomotion of her little body, made me guilt-sick. Her whole life was my fault.

We went down into the station. Bea took her place naturally among the crowd on the platform, tilting her head to push in her earbuds, hunched over with the rest of them. Then I was alone with Richie Dee, the busker. I knew his name because it was printed on the sign at his feet, along with various social media and cash app handles. Down at mid-platform, Richie slid to a soft falsetto at the high reaches of "Take On Me," picking a folky pattern on his guitar. Every morning he wore that patched denim jacket; his hair curtained his face as he sang. Richie Dee was a studied ironist, his song selections contrived,

I supposed, to feel novel to the early hour and his spare arrangements. A cheap joke, but his guitar case was always full of dollars he'd charmed from the crowd.

Light bloomed along the far curve of the tunnel wall. The train arrived.

"I'll see you tonight?" Bea squeezed my hand, looked into my eyes. Then she turned with the rest and pushed toward the car. The violence in that surge of bodies was only latent, though I sensed in it a template you could use to understand some moment, yet to come, when things would be more desperate, for one reason or another. Someone told me once that the police commonly find strange packages on the train, or in the stations or tunnels, dry runs of some kind, maybe coordinated. They keep a log, when and where and what's been found: brand-new backpacks filled with, for example, nails or ball bearings. It was now just a quarter past seven—I tended to think that anyone, after all that planning, would wait for the peak of the rush. Then again, maybe that sort of logic was out-of-date.

The train sang into motion. Richie Dee and I kept our eyes down and apart, and the platform began to fill again.

3

Back up on the avenue, I stopped under the green awning of the Mesa, the little diner where lately I'd been going to see Aggie. She worked the third shift, clocked out at eight, and there was something charming in the way we crossed from opposite directions, Aggie having come through the long, fluorescent overnight, me still waking up. The end of her shift, in sunlight, made her giddy; at that hour I was slow. We shared the incongruity like a joke.

A man appeared on the sidewalk beside me, cocked his head to catch my eye, asked if I was going in. He pushed past and opened the door. Through the plate glass I watched him take a counter seat, brush aside the sugar shaker, pull the napkin close. And then there was Aggie, coffeepot in hand, pausing now before the guy to right the mug on his paper place mat and fill it. She reminded me of a pug, her stocky middle, the way her legs moved under the green apron. And she was strikingly short. I'd guess not much over five feet. She wore her hair buzzed close; she was pale-skinned, with a stud in her left nostril and gray eyes set wide in a thick, ruddy face. Aggie was or had been a graduate student, though I couldn't recall the field, something intellectual and unlucrative. But if any part of her held me in disdain—for my age, my business attire, or for working in private equity, sucking the money from the middle of the world—she didn't show it. She must have been in her late twenties, twelve or fifteen years older than Bea, and in some deep inarticulate way I'd come to think of the two of them as in conversation: Talking to Aggie felt like talking to Bea, the way personalities commingle in dreams. I watched her with the man at the counter, laughing, growing serious, nodding dearly. He wore a blue suit, must have been on his way into town, and I had the sense of seeing myself, or the person I might have been on another day.

"I'll tell you a story, Walter," Aggie had said the last time I'd entered the Mesa, maybe two weeks earlier. "This is true. Ready? Overnight, one thirty or so, this guy walks in and sits down right there." I'd followed her eyes to an empty booth, duct tape spanning a tear in the green vinyl. "He had this fastidious way about him, like a neatness in his motions, very polite, a little too formal. Real tall and skinny. Black guy. With a mustache just right here across the top of his lip. He had on a gray topcoat and red scarf, and he didn't take either off. He ordered a cheeseburger, no bun, no fries. And when it came—like as soon as I put the plate down, it must know to wait for the sound—this tiny dog popped out of the front pocket of the coat. Just its head. A Chihuahua maybe, or, I don't know, smaller than that even. And it had this guy's same vibe, like very proper as its head popped out. The guy cut the cheese-burger up with a knife and fork and fed the whole thing, bite by bite, to the dog." And she gawked in wonder to signal the anecdote's end.

An experiment, I guessed, should have a method. Aggie made me feel good, or normal, at least, like anyone else drinking coffee in a diner. I left her there in the window and turned up the avenue.

When I passed our street, I was thinking about Nora. How simple it should have been to find her in the kitchen, listening to the news through her phone, brewing coffee to take in her travel mug on the train, asking as I hung up my keys how Bea had seemed. She was on Madison near Fifty-Seventh Street when she died. Headed south, toward the F train. It was February, early evening. There had been a snowstorm that morning, the only one of the season. Everything the police had said on the phone I'd had to repeat as a question. I put my finger in the other ear to block the street noise. I started looking for a cab.

4

The sun was chalky and dull, and the end of the morning commute felt like low tide, everything washed out into the city. Broken parking meters stood lined up like an execution, yellow bags over their heads. There was an optometrist, a jeweler. The bus passed again and again. For so long, I'd never missed a day of work, and to be in that place at that time on a weekday was subtly but profoundly strange.

I didn't know what I was doing; I had no clear sense as to what I hoped might happen. I had dressed only for the walk to the train in flip-flops, college sweatpants, and my winter coat, zipped over an undershirt. I felt something as I walked, though, and it was more than just the novelty of self-determination, or that early, chilly sense of the day as a blank slate. It was a pull, like it wasn't me that was walking, exactly, but the force, or whatever you'd call it—the thing that the experiment was intended to focus and amplify. I myself was just observing.

But by the time I'd wandered another mile or so, I felt absurd and ashamed. My mind kept veering back along the path I was meant to have taken, to the city, the office, to Len, my father-in-law. And to Denton Whitwell, the investment manager Len had hired to consult with us that week. For months, it had loomed on the firm's calendar. Denton was one of the most brilliant minds in finance, and to secure that kind of access to him was no small feat. You had to inch your way toward him, there were politics involved. So seldom was he wrong about where the money wanted to go that a culture of joking worship had sprung up around him. People in our world fawned over Denton Whitwell, ironically ascribed witchy powers to him. Len did it, too. Denton was a money genius, there was no denying that, but I'd never liked him: his carved-pumpkin smirk, his enormous body, the imperious decadence it suggested. I'd just always had a feeling about him.

At the next intersection, I lingered without crossing. To know that Denton and Len were far from me, afloat in that nest of tall buildings cordoned off by the river, occasioned alternating waves of terror and relief. Len had made so many excuses for me that year already. If I hurried back, I could still make the afternoon meeting. It might mean all the difference. Cold shower, Sudafed, clean suit. Afterward, I could text Bea. The two of us could have dinner in the city.

An ambulance passed, lights on but no siren.

I should go, I thought. I should go home right now.

And then I saw the strangest thing: a dog, enormous, a white komondor, trotting across the avenue, masterless and unleashed, dirty locks swaying, coming straight for me. There were no cars, but that's not why I hadn't any sense that the dog was in danger. It was because the dog was so calm and assured, moving as if the avenue were a shallow brook in a wide plain in some remote country. It felt like we were the only two living things for miles, and when it reached me—high as my waist, I looked straight down into its coffee-colored eyes—it paused, dipped its head, and swung it firmly into my left hip. I yielded.

The dog padded down the block, turned the corner, and was gone.

Then, off to my left, someone called, "Daniel? So sorry! I'm never late, I swear."

It was a young man, olive-complected with a close-clipped beard. As he approached, he fished in the pocket of his slim wool coat, head cocked in concentration, and then pulled out a set of keys. "Pardon me," he said, motioning to a door I hadn't realized I was blocking. He tried one key, then another. I summoned my breath to speak but only a croak issued; I winced, put my hands to my throat. "Oh my goodness," he said, "under the weather?" He clucked his tongue. "And just since we spoke on the phone? There's something nasty going around, there really is. We had it in the office. I seem to have been spared. Knock wood." The third key worked. He pushed the door open, held it with his foot, leaned back, looked in either direction and then straight up the building's face. "No wood? There's wood upstairs. I'll be fine." He laughed, walked inside, held the door.

For an instant, I hesitated; I almost made to protest.

Inside there were mailboxes, one broken and ajar, and takeout menus on the floor. On a cork message board, a handwritten note about the washing machine in the basement: cold water only. I touched the banister where the stairs landed, turned back and looked out onto the street, feeling slightly outside myself. The building had always been there. And now I had been—what? Granted access, was the phrase that suggested itself. I started up the stairs, a little spellbound.

On the fifth floor the man opened a door marked 5A and said, with a note of quiet apology, "The tenant's out, but they leave the TV on for the cat." Beige wall-to-wall carpeting, a tattered blond couch, a black beanbag chair. In the tiny kitchen, a white range, rust-spotted and ancient. Beside the television—a shopping network, played loud— sat a litter box. Blue grains of litter lay atop the knits in the carpet around it. A Chinese wall calendar hung by the refrigerator. The place was aromatic with old cooking and unfamiliar cleaning products.

The man took a sharp breath. "Well—for the distance to the train you can't beat it. Two bedrooms. Here, follow me." As he walked, he tapped out a text message.

In the first bedroom, I pulled the maroon duvet down from the pillows. He frowned, glanced at me sidelong, bent to pull it back. "Now, this way," he said, leading me down a short hall, "is the second bedroom. It's smaller, but not the worst you're going to see in this neighborhood." He opened a door onto an unfurnished room, warm with light and full of boxes. "They use it for storage, but it's not a bad space. Nice view onto the avenue." I leaned over the window and looked out. "Take your time," he said. "I'll meet you back out front."

There was a cardboard box filled with children's toys, books, photos, some loose, some framed. I picked one up: two teenagers, Chinese, on prom night, both in braces, he in a gleaming tuxedo, she in purple with a blue corsage. I set it back. Then I started digging through the box. There was a rubber-band ball, an old hard drive. There was a big red dictionary, the old-fashioned kind. And then there was something I recognized at once, though only a corner jutted from the pile. It was a miniature watercolor, four by six, of the Manhattan skyline. In the painting, set in a simple wooden frame, late-afternoon sun spilled over the buildings in soft brushstrokes. I knew it because the view was from our rooftop. Nora had painted the picture. For years it had hung in our bedroom. After she died, I'd left it out on the stoop—along with a few others she'd done, and some of her shoes, and a stack of novels, annotated in pencil, that she'd kept since college. All of it was gone within an hour. Bea, when she found out, wouldn't speak to me. Now I slipped the painting into my coat. And when I turned, there was the cat, black with green eyes, watching from atop a cardboard box.

The agent was in the kitchen. He looked up from his phone. "I'm showing it quite a bit. It'll go fast. Take my card."

## 5

I made my way down wide arteries and narrow side streets, through empty lots, in and out of sunlight, wired and jittery, feeling exposed to unfamiliar elements. Had I been made to commit—if I'd passed an acquaintance, for example, and the acquaintance had asked what I had in my coat—I would have shrugged it off. The weirdest coincidence. A comic misunderstanding. And I did believe that. In the most literal sense, it was the truth. But it was also true, or seemed or felt true, that something was *happening*—the process that had been unfolding all week had now accelerated. Wasn't the proof right there in my coat, sticking into my ribs? I could answer no to that question, go home, and get back in bed. But that thought was intolerable to me. So alternatively, I could keep moving. Try not to look it in the eye. If I just didn't think too hard, maybe I could keep the ball in the air.

I crossed and recrossed the street, made impulsive turns, looking only at the ground. I was thinking about Bea. I saw us as two blue dots on a map. Here I was, and at just that moment she might have been seated behind a folding desk, copying equations or grammar rules from the white board. On the admissions tour, just fourteen months earlier, Nora and I had stood together, peering into those classrooms, invited by our guide to imagine Bea among the girls there. There were good schools closer to home, I'd argued; Bea didn't need to travel so far. But Nora had attended the school herself, and Len sat on the board.

Now the air felt weird and clammy, unseasonably humid, and with one hand on the frame in my coat it was easy to imagine that some real state of parity existed between my rising fever and the weather itself. I should run, I thought, and so I tried, though in the flip-flops I could only manage an awkward trot. Briefly I worried about the way I'd look to someone watching from a window, but that was a conventional sensibility, and anyway, I soon had to stop on the corner, shivering and sputtering, hands on my thighs. I wiped my nose with my sleeve, took a deep breath, stood tall again to fill my lungs. I stayed there a short while, my mind a total blank. And then I saw that dog—the same one, the white komondor, trotting up the block from my right.

The dog watched me coolly as it neared, and now it occurred to me to wonder just what it was doing, exactly, wandering all alone. Here it was. It sniffed me without stopping as it passed, and I watched it cross the street, tail held high, feet rising and falling like pistons.

The dog kept twenty yards ahead as I followed past brownstones and bodegas, past men sleeping in double-parked cars. She—looked like a she, I thought—was quick. I had to move to keep up, and my breathing grew ragged, my chest throbbed and felt septic. Part of me wished I could call out, but to say what? *Please, just one moment!* Together we traveled past the southern lip of the park, then onto the covered walk that stretched over the highway, the air smutty with exhaust, and out past the cemetery, where the buildings grew squatter and lonelier. I couldn't help thinking of Nora: if she could see me now. I often thought that way about her. If I could only talk to her—if she could just tell me what to do. But the farther we went, the more sense it made, because once you've accepted that you're following the dog, you're free to forget it and focus in at the granular level: making a light to cross the street, or skirting a construction site.

Finally, the dog pranced up the steps of a large prewar apartment building. It began to bark. When the door buzzed, the dog nosed it open. I caught it as it fell.

The atrium was lightless, acrid with old smoke. At the sound of a door unlatching above, the dog threw its weight unevenly up the stairs. I felt nervous; automatically, I began generating excuses for myself. Then a voice called, "Tilly! Come here! Where's my good girl? You have a nice walk?"

I tracked the sound with my eyes and saw her leaning out over the second-floor railing: Aggie. She shrieked and clapped her hands.

## 6

At the Mesa, Aggie and I mainly spoke of what was before us—the weather, the neighborhood. But there had been one exception. On a Friday between Christmas and New Year's, I found myself sitting up, avoiding sleep. Bea was at Len's, and there in the empty house, late at night, I'd been beset by this restless, lonely feeling. I drank some, then too much, and briefly I felt light and good, playing music loud. Around two o'clock, I realized I was famished.

I'd never seen the Mesa that way, so deep in its night-time life, lit up like a beacon. Aggie was on, as I'd known she would be. She brought me coffee without asking, and I ordered a cheeseburger. The place was like a theater after the crowd's gone, the actors smoking cigarettes. Salsa music floated through the kitchen door, propped open with a yellow mop bucket. I remember the pale flip sides of the window decorations, snowflakes, wreaths, and mistletoe.

The Mesa didn't serve alcohol, but Aggie gave me an Amstel Light and opened one for herself. It was the first time Aggie and I spoke about Nora, though of course she already knew. Pictures of the aftermath—the black smoke and green flames—spread across social media when it happened, and headlines about our ongoing lawsuits still cropped up now and then. I don't like to describe those things, but that night at the Mesa, I did tell Aggie some of how I felt. About my fixation, for example, on the idea that our miserable present, Bea's and mine, had assembled itself from the materials of a past in which we'd been so blithely happy. All our lives, we'd been untouched by hardship or tragedy. But our future without Nora must have been written all around us from the start—I was convinced of that, even if I couldn't say why. And so my thinking about time had changed. I no longer conceived of the future as something remote from me, there in the present; I felt certain that we had coexisted with Nora's death before it happened in ways I hadn't understood. I often found myself wondering what even grimmer futures were contained in or written on all that surrounded me now— the dark and disordered mess of stalagmites I sometimes saw above my head or through the window. What else was coming down the pike?

In the morning, I found a guest check from the Mesa in my pocket. There were no charges, only a 647 number, written in green ink and underlined, and the word *whenever*. Seeing it, hungover, I flushed and felt sick—she'd taken pity on me; maybe she'd thought I'd need help getting home. I scanned my memory and found no major gaps: We talked, and then I'd walked back to the house. That was all. Still, I was too old. I had to take a hard look at my drinking. I had no business unburdening myself like that to a near stranger who was just trying to get through her shift.

I waited until after New Year's to apologize. But when I took my seat at the Mesa, Aggie appeared with my bowl of cornflakes, smiling, like nothing had ever happened. Watching her walk off behind the counter, I felt such gratitude that my eyes welled.

7

Now she stood in the doorway, barefoot, in mesh shorts and a gray hooded sweatshirt. Her toes were stout and sprouted just lightly with a few delicate hairs. She regarded me, I thought, in something like awe, and I found myself scanning the space anxiously for the green Mesa apron, or any other grounding, familiar sight.

It was a studio, cramped and far too hot even with all the windows open. A flannel sleeping bag covered a mattress on the floor, the counter was heaped with dishes and takeout containers, clothes lay everywhere. Entering, I stepped over a toppled sneaker whose mate I spotted later in the bathroom. Everywhere, in piles and stacks and splayed underfoot, were books—creased paperbacks, fat anthologies, readers, philosophy, history, literature, criticism.

"Walter," Aggie said. She was close now; she took hold of my arm. "Man—you look like shit." I coughed into my fist, put my hand to my throat, and mouthed: *My voice.* I felt like a child; my cheeks burned. "Oh, no!" she said, wide-eyed. "*Walter.*" It was just the way she said it at the Mesa, one high note and one low, soft and full of care. She came closer, wheeled me nimbly around, guided me onto the mattress. Her movements were somehow both clumsy and sure, and looking into her face, I felt certain she hadn't been to bed. She parted her legs, settled onto me, and pushed her mouth onto mine, taking my face in her hands, kissing my cheeks and down my neck and back up to my ear, whispering, "It's okay, it's okay, it's okay." She leaned back to untie my sweatpants, and I came unfrozen, feeling now that I wanted this, because I would say yes to anything the experiment set forth for me, here, and now here, and now here. But then something in me collapsed. Aggie must have felt it. She paused, lifted her head, and looked at me. I hadn't been with anyone since Nora.

"Don't worry," Aggie said, falling onto the mattress and draping an arm across me. "We'll have more time."

The remark seemed cryptic.

Tilly circled and hunkered against the mattress. I wondered briefly if Aggie might fall asleep, but she drew a breath, patted my chest, heaved herself up, removed the gym shorts, and pulled on a pair of jeans. She reached for a pill bottle that lay beside the bed, shook out an orange tablet, crushed it on the back of a textbook with the ashtray, swept it into a line and sniffed it up, then sat back, rubbing her nose.

"Sorry," she said, clearing her throat. "I don't mean to be, like, disgusting. It's my Dexedrine. They'll only give it to me in time-release but it works better this way." Then with a lighter she opened two beer bottles and gave one to me. The taste was a shock, so early and in my state. She put water in Tilly's dish, lit a cigarette, whirled around the tiny apartment, stuffing things into a large backpack: two bottles of whiskey, more cigarettes, three packs of pita bread and a block of cheese and half a Saran-wrapped deli ham that must have come from the Mesa.

"This is too weird!" she said. "But whatever. There's no such thing as a coincidence, so everything is automatically perfect. Because what's the alternative—you know what I mean? But look, we've got to move, let's go, we cannot miss the train!"

When she came near to ash her cigarette, I took her by the wrist. *Where?* I mouthed. "Oh—to see Lucca Castle." And when I stared, she repeated: "Lucca Castle."

My tongue moved to shape the words. Lucca Castle—I didn't know what that was. A person, or a place.

"Do you need anything from your house?" she asked. "We'd have to hurry, but I don't know, a change of clothes, or a toothbrush?"

I thought about Bea. Two blue dots. In the cafeteria, maybe, a carton of milk on her red plastic tray, or some crackers in packets. She never ate her lunch, the school nurse had told me on the phone that autumn.

Aggie looked at my feet. "Shoes?"

## 8

Aggie's steps were quick. So were her eyes. She hadn't slept, and she was high. I guessed I'd never known her all that well. Now, as Tilly walked ahead of us, Aggie talked about Lucca Castle, but it didn't pass for an explanation. She leapt between topics, spoke familiarly of people I didn't know. We were going to a party, she said. All her friends wanted to meet me, and they were—here, I became confused—performance artists, or activists, or academics, or all of those things. It sounded like Aggie had been this Lucca Castle's student, or she still was, only now in some less formal capacity, because he'd been fired from Queens College, I guess, after distributing psychedelics to his students. Aggie spoke of that situation with real bitterness as *political*. She kept taking and kissing my hand, insisting I'd love Lucca. He was brilliant, you could listen to him all night, the crowds were bigger all the time. And he was very interested in me. I looked at her. "Well—because I told him all about you. And our talk that night. What you said was beautiful." She reddened. "Anyway, Lucca asked me to bring you out. You two can help each other. You'll see. He can explain things to you. A sudden loss like yours functions more or less as a rite of initiation. That's what Lucca says."

We retraced the route I'd made earlier with Bea, down the steps and into the subway, but now there was something odd—a loud hum, coming from farther underground. It had force, it rang in my chest, and half-way down the tunnel, unsure what it was, I slowed and grabbed Aggie's arm. "Hey, come on," she said, pulling free. "We can't miss this train, I'm telling you." But the sound rattled my teeth. By the time I reached the stairs, it was nearly unbearable; the sound rang in my eyeballs, my tongue. I held tight to the railing, took one step at a time. And when I reached the platform, there it was: Richie Dee. The acoustic was packed up, case shut and tip sign gone, and, with an electric, he leaned over a pedal board, rocking back and forth, the only soul now in the station. He struck the guitar's body with a closed fist, shook the neck. There were no individually discernible sounds, only the roar. Aggie and Richie nodded familiarly at each other, and then she and Tilly made down toward the platform's end, their footsteps inaudible under the noise.

Richie Dee looked up at me, once, quickly. The sound snaked down the tunnel and flew back. I stood there, studying him, hardly noticing the garbage train creeping into the station—yellow barge cars pulled by an old Redbird. I took its arrival to mean we'd have a while to wait. But then, over Richie's shoulder, I saw Aggie waving frantically at me, leaning from inside the last car.

## 9

"Dead hairstyles," said Aggie, peering at the faces in an ad for a defunct radio station. The train must have been twenty years out of service. She took a seat, yawning. "You might as well make yourself comfortable. This thing's slow as shit." She reclined, stretched her legs over the bench; I relaxed into her arms, and she played in my hair with her hands.

We were quiet.

After a while, she said, "I'll tell you a story." She spoke dreamily, her right hand hanging to rub Tilly under the neck. She seemed to have come down some. "When I was a kid, after my dad died, I could hear what people were thinking. The first time was with Mrs. Carter, in fourth grade. One day I got in trouble—I don't remember for what; I was always in trouble then, you know—and I had to skip recess and clean the chalkboard. Mrs. Carter was sitting behind me at her desk, looking out the window. Down below was the blacktop where the kids played. And as I was wiping the board, I heard her. Behind me. Like, I

*felt* her. I remember staring at this one line of chalk, paralyzed. It wasn't words, it wasn't anything I could repeat.
It was like a cloud inside the room: She was so, so sad. I
turned to look. Mrs. Carter had big red hair that she wore
up, old-fashioned, and pearl glasses, and that day she was
in a purple cardigan. Without thinking of it or meaning
to, I asked my dad what to do. And he said, *It's allowed.*
There were times when I knew I'd invented the words my
dad said to me, and times I knew they were real. And this
was real. So I walked over to her desk. She looked down
and said, in this far-off voice, like she'd forgotten she was
supposed to be punishing me, 'All finished, Agatha?' And I
put my hand on top of her hand, on the armrest of her old
wooden rolling chair. For a second it was weird. But then
she relaxed and put her other hand on top of mine, and
she looked back out the window, and we stood that way
together." The train rolled past lamps recessed in the tunnel walls. Their light hit the front of the car, slid across us
and out the back. "I don't remember how it ended. I don't
know what happened to Mrs. Carter."

Aggie kissed the crown of my head. Then, running her
hand along my side, she caught the edge of the frame.
"What's this?"

I opened my coat. Together we looked at the painting.
"Fuck, man," she said, very softly. "You even brought a
binding agent." I didn't know what that meant. But when
she asked if I'd painted it, I shook my head. "It's real
pretty," she said. It was. The city so clean and bright. I
could feel Nora's presence in the scene she'd rendered,

like she might still be there on the other side of the canvas, if only there was a way of turning your head to see her. My eyes grew heavy. I thought about Bea. I tried to remember the last time she fell asleep in my arms, the way I'd soon fall asleep in Aggie's. I couldn't. But there had been a last time, just as there'd been a final night beside Nora, and I wished that everything would die together, all at once, and not by turns.

## 10

After work, Len liked to go to his social club, in a stately townhouse with a sweeping marble staircase, named reading rooms, a coat-check girl you weren't allowed to tip. In my early days at the firm, he'd sometimes bring me along. If it happened to be a Tuesday, we'd go upstairs after supper to play cards. "Do you know, Walter," said the fat, pockmarked man running the table on the first occasion I played, "you are about to join the oldest poker game in the New World?" Under the hanging brass lamps he shuffled the deck. "Every Tuesday night, continuously, since 1841. Now the way things shake out, a lot'll happen on a Tuesday. For example, there've been twenty-six games held on Christmas. But then too—well, the invasion of Normandy began on a Tuesday morning."

Someone else offered: "Every presidential election since 1848."

Another: "Crash of '29."

"*Challenger.*"

"9/11."

He began to deal. "We've been here through it all," he said, ironically theatrical, "and whatsoever should befall us next Tuesday, Walter, and the one after that, and the one after that, we'll be here then."

This was Denton Whitwell.

Len admired Denton quite nakedly. Because he was richer, certainly—richer than anyone else at the club—and better connected. Denton moved more formidably through our world and, too, into loftier spheres: He had the ear of the governor; he dined with heads of state; he was one of the world's most prodigious collectors of modern art. A reader of Greek and Latin, Denton counted many friends in academia and, every other spring, taught a course at Columbia on international affairs.

Twice a year or so Denton would announce an informal evening lecture at the club on the global economy. We'd sit in Hepplewhite chairs and drink Japanese scotch as Denton leaned on a podium there by the hearth, jacket and no tie, painting a picture of things to come. And then he'd take questions. What about drones? AI? Climate change—what were they saying behind closed doors? What about all this bunker-building? Where will we be in a quarter century? Or fifteen years, or ten? How do we get ready? How much longer, really, do we have? That, I sensed, was the final question, but it was never asked, not in so many words, and if Denton knew, he didn't say.

In the mail one day I received a bid for membership at the club. Len was annoyed and embarrassed when I declined. It's just too far from home, I'd told him, and that was part of the truth. But the rest of it would have been harder to explain: That I didn't want to be pulled any farther into that world than I already had been. And that, in hindsight, each maneuver I'd made toward it—out-of-state school, business degree, the requisite eighty-hour weeks at my first associate position—felt almost unconscious, or reflexive, like I could detail that trajectory but not wholly account for it. And to hear myself speak the language of business so fluently still felt strange. I didn't know if that was really me, my voice, or whether I'd become more like an avatar for something else. In reverie I'd see it, the firm, as an enormous tethered balloon, all of us holding the ropes, like in a parade. One morning at the Mesa, Aggie had asked what sorts of investments we made. I was surprised at how unwelcome I'd found the question. Stumbling through my answer, I looked into my cereal, circling the bowl with my spoon. The job held little of my interest or imagination. I didn't want to talk about it.

Len was a good man. His pleasures in life were simple. But his devotion to work was unironic and uncritical, and maybe that's why some small, strangled part of him had felt proud that Denton flew back from Hong Kong to attend Nora's funeral service. Denton had approached me there, placed one hand on my back and the other around my wrist, and told me how beautiful she'd been. He called her a beautiful creature. Then he moved on to Bea. Bent to push her hair aside, spoke softly in her ear. Everyone watched him, seemed fascinated by him; when he was in the room, people measured their reactions against his. Denton was past sixty, but there were rumors about his private life. At the club, those closest to him even got away with knowing wisecracks and dark intimations. He'd shrug and grin boyishly: "I'm a committed bachelor. I have no attachments to honor, as some of you may."

My eyes were closed, head in Aggie's lap. The train scraped along. I could see Denton and Len, seated beside each other, at a conference table, in a small room high in the air. And then, half asleep, the scenes tangling in my head, I saw Denton in the cathedral, head bowed, one hand on the lid of Nora's casket.

## 11

Aggie was gently stroking my cheek. "This is it," she said. The train had slowed. Visible through the windows on either side were sparse woods, the trees craggy and dead under a blank sky. Aggie stood and walked to the rear door, which had never fully closed, squeezed through and hopped down. Tilly and I followed. Feet planted in the pale, sandy soil, we watched the train lumber off.

Tilly turned down a thin trail into the trees, bounding and crashing through the brush; she'd disappear and then leap out to urge us on, tongue lolling. The ground sucked at my shoes. There was an odor of dirty water and black mud, thinned to winter. Overhead, gulls called.

Weird spot for a party.

"Here," Aggie said, and through a break in the trees I saw a beach, sand and water the same dull shade. It was a dead, uncatalogued place, crowded with refuse. Spread before us in the sand was old china, rusted paint cans, car parts, broken umbrellas, toilet seats, lamps, suitcases, luggage, keys, books, shoes, and, throughout, dark, porous fragments, like charcoal or petrified wood. Aggie fished one of these out of the sand. It was a bone. "There used to be a rendering plant out here, a hundred years ago or more. There are horse bones everywhere still. Look, here, a skull." She picked it up, shook the sand from its mouth. The teeth jigsawed up the side in a grin. "He wants to give you a kiss," she said, pressing it at me, and instinctually I swatted at the thing. It broke in two at the jaw's hinge and hit the sand with a silken sound. Aggie clucked her tongue, buried her hands in the pockets of her sweatshirt as a cold wind blew off the water: "And that's how you repay his affections." She set her eyes on a point up the beach. "Up here," she said, "there's a shelter." I could dimly make it out: a lean-to built of corrugated sheeting.

Ahead of us, Tilly spread her legs to defecate, straightened, kicked sand out behind her, and nosed around until she came up carrying, in her teeth, a dark length of bone.

The shelter was decorated like some dockside bar with an old sofa of a dirty mustard suede, empty liquor bottles, and scavenged things—lockets, antique silverware. Aggie hunkered down with a shiver. The bones, once you saw to pick them out, were everywhere. "Here," she said, wiping her mouth with her sleeve and offering an uncapped bottle of whiskey. I took the bottle and swigged from it. A cold wind ripped up the beach.

She pointed across the water. "That's it, by the way."

A sailing yacht sat anchored just offshore, rolling atop the waves.

I guessed I should feel something, looking at it: the experiment's terminus. But I was ill, exhausted, increasingly numbed to the day's strangeness.

Aggie sat forward, looked into the distance, stood up. "Oh, cool. That's bound to be Hector and Sim."

She placed her fingers in her mouth and whistled, and then we fell silent, awaiting the two approaching figures—young and rugged, carrying backpacks, dressed something like street kids or militiamen in black, tan, and olive. Hector was slender and dark, Hispanic, I thought, with a rough beard and messy curls. As he neared the lean-to, he eyed me with an arch smile. Sim's complexion was Irish. He looked wiry and mean, thin lipped and gaunt cheeked, with reddish hair clipped close, like Aggie's. Pearls dangled from both of his ears. He ducked under the roof of the lean-to and stood like a buzzard, thumbs hooked under the straps of his backpack.

"You're drinking already?" he said.

"You're late," said Aggie. "We were bored. And I worked all fucking night, man."

"Well, who the fuck is this?" said Sim.

"It's her guy," said Hector, grinning. "What's-his-name."

"That's him?" Sim said, eyes on Aggie and pointing at me.

Aggie said, "Yeah, this is Walter, and he's mine—don't you try and take any credit with Lucca for recruiting him." Petulantly, she stuck out her tongue.

Hector sat down hard in the sand, clasped his hands around his knees. "We're glad you came, Walter."

"Anyway," said Aggie, "I barely *had* to recruit him. He just showed up at my house, dude, spooky as fuck. Scout's fucking honor. Right, Walter?"

Sim said, "What's the matter, doesn't he talk?"

Aggie placed a hand on my arm. "No, man, as a matter of fact, he's got laryngitis or something. Anyway, Walter's cool. I vouch." She kicked up her legs, rolled back into the cushions. "On the couch, I vouch. I vouch on the couch, you—you slouching grouch!" Then she said, "Oh, hey, check this out—he even brought a binding agent. Show them, Walter."

I pulled Nora's painting from my coat. They stared at it, then fell into talk I didn't bother trying to follow. I reached to take the whiskey from where it sat in the sand. Where was Bea? In my mind, I conjured her: now at basketball practice, in the drafty gym, cutting through a maze of orange cones.

Sim was filling buckets with sand. Hector walked up the beach to pull a graying canoe from the brush.

I leaned back, closed my eyes. The whole year had been such a wilderness.

## 12

I'd half expected the cabin door of the *Pop! Goes the Weasel*—the yacht's name, lettered in gold across a midnight-blue hull that leaned smartly into each passing wave—to open onto maybe a field of stars. Someone whose name I'd gathered was Carla would descend now and then to confer with Lucca. She said he was still sort of waking up. Tall and balletic, dark-skinned, her long braids tied back, Carla had appeared on the deck to throw us a rope as we'd approached in the canoe—Aggie and I seated together in the middle, Hector and Sim rowing at either end, and in the prow Tilly, standing tall. Like Washington, Hector had joked. A handful of others lounged topside, reading, sleeping; they noted me with the barest interest.

To the west, the city wore a lavender sheen. Night was coming. My fever felt high. I was a little drunk. Everything seemed to pass through a long corridor on its way to my senses. And when, finally, we were called to descend through the cabin door, I moved as if in a dream. This was it. Inside was dim, lit only by an electric lantern that hung over the long, low table in the center of the space, and in every flimsy surface to which I put my hand was the give and sway of the bay beneath us. The thin carpeting smelled of old seawater and cleaning chemicals. Along three sides of the table were built-in benches, vinyl-cushioned, and seated at its head was, I presumed, Lucca Castle. Slight and unshaven, pallid, with tired eyes and a black hooded sweatshirt zipped tight to the neck. He wore the sullen, distracted air of someone caught up in a long struggle to wrestle down some vast idea. Here and there his black hair showed gray. I guessed he was near to my age. We slid into place around him, lamplight falling on our foreheads and cheekbones to make dark hollows of our eyes. Like the skull on the beach. No one spoke. Then Aggie cleared her throat, fished in her pocket for a Dexedrine, and crushed it on the table. Lucca watched, impassive, as she sorted the pile and sniffed it up. She threw her head back, coughed, rubbed her face, and pulled air roughly through her nose, three times fast.

Lucca hunched forward, pursed his lips, rubbed his stubbled cheeks. "What, uh," he said, then slapped his hands on the table and sat back again. "What time is it?"

No one answered.

"Never mind," he said, "I don't care. I love you all. You know that? Even this guy." He shook a finger at me. "I don't know who the fuck you are, man, but—"

"This is Walter," Aggie broke in eagerly, taking my hand in hers. "Walter." And when he only stared, she added: "Remember? The guy I told you about, my customer . . ."

Lucca blinked. "I remember only ideas and sensations."

She gripped my hand tighter. "He's the one—the guy you said—the private equity guy—the guy whose wife . . ."

And his face changed. "Oh," he said. "Oh. Oh! Yeah." He nodded. "Yeah, yeah, yeah, yeah, yeah, yeah, yeah. Right on. Walter." He waved his hand sinuously over Aggie, in blessing. "Excellent work, Agent Agatha." Then he appraised me. "Walter. Okay. You look like shit, man."

Aggie touched my knee. "He can't talk. He's got laryngitis or something."

Lucca shrugged. "Fine. Get well soon, Walter." Then he sighed and bowed his head. Around me, everyone did the same. Aggie nudged me with an elbow, and I saw that they'd all joined hands.

"A moment," he said, "of consciously directed intention toward our success. Hail to the ancient dreams."

And with the others I closed my eyes. There was Bea—shivering in the locker room, pulling on her kilt and cream cashmere sweater. On the train, legs crossed, waiting for her phone to refresh at Thirty-Fourth Street, then Twenty-Third, then Fourteenth. Texting to ask how I felt, to make plans for dinner, receiving no reply. Pushing through the revolving doors off Union Square and taking the elevator to Dr. Harper's office, to spend one more hour there on the task of assimilating the past year into a functional life.

"Walter," said Lucca. "Come sit with me."

Aggie slid up over my lap so I could move toward him, and they all started in on some project: Sim disappeared into the hold and returned with a stack of shallow plastic trays; Carla opened a bag of cement; Hector carried buckets of bay water into the cabin from up top.

"Walter," Lucca said again, pulling his ankles up to sit cross-legged, yawning, rolling his neck. "You know, I sort of thought you'd be taller. You looked taller, I mean, in that picture in the *Times*."

Their hands were moving, mixing cement and the sand we'd brought from the beach—thick with bone, glass, and metal—together in the trays, pouring bay water over them.

"It's terrible what happened, Walter. I'm very sorry about it. Though of course that sort of thing isn't as rare as one might think. Well, you probably know that, now. You of all people." He took my hand in his, turned it over, began to stroke my wrist with his thumb. "The city's a dangerous place. Pedestrian fatalities are up. So are train deaths. There's falling debris, manhole explosions, rusted-through cellar doors swallowing people whole. But it's more than that. The fabric's wearing thin. Everyone's afraid of one another. You can feel it; everybody knows it—it's all going to shit out there."

They were scraping the wet cement level with spackles.

"But you've come to the right place. So, look," he said and cleared his throat, "if you begin from the assumption that the city is not a human space—that the city is an outgrowth of the twin forces of capital and technology, which have now developed beyond our ability to control them—and that, *to* the city, the bodies it contains are just so much raw material with which to generate profit . . ."

He trailed off, looked up at me, and when I only stared back, said, "Well, come on, man—this isn't, like, breaking news. Look, Walter, I get that your line of work doesn't exactly reward a lot of deep thinking. But over the past year, you must have done some. That's why you're here. Have you ever stopped and asked yourself who, or what, it is that you really work for? If your shareholders want constant, unchecked growth, and that growth is lethal to humans—I mean, you see what I'm getting at, don't you? Economic and technological development are a form of mass suicide. We know that. So how do we understand the *impulse* toward it? Who's driving the train? See, to me, that's the mystery." I'd let my eyes lose focus, listening to his voice and the rapping and scratching of the tools in their hands. "I don't know what to call it, exactly. The train-driver. But I do know that it's some force, or spirit, or intelligence. It's not human, though to manifest itself in our world, it makes use of human hands. Capital, technology, industry—those are its expressions, but they're not *it*. Who knows. Maybe it's an extraterrestrial virus. Some kind of parasite. Maybe it's demonic. I believe that it's sentient. But on the question of what exactly it *wants*, Walter, I'm of several minds. Does it just want to kill us, render the planet uninhabitable? Maybe. But it could be that its aims are stranger. Unimaginable to us, even. Let's say we survive to do this thing's bidding for another thousand years. What's that look like? If it's using us to build itself, like, *what* are we building? You know what I mean? What happens when the process is *complete*?"

He let go of my wrist and pulled himself into a lotus position. "I believe that us humans can stop it. Kneecap this thing. We're obligated to try, anyhow. Of course, it'll have to be a buzzer-beater. It's got us by the balls, man. The only way out is down." He made his hand into a pistol, put it to his temple, and mimed the hammer falling. "So when I advocate mass destruction, Walter, understand that I'm advocating only the acceleration of an inevitable process. We're past the point of no return. All we can do is hit the gas. Try and push the system to collapse before this thing gets whatever it is that it wants. Then the ragged handful left standing can pick up the pieces. Start fresh. It's a bummer, yeah, but there you have it."

They shook and rocked the trays, banged them against the table to bring air bubbles to the surface.

"Look," he said, "we're not terrorists. Our method is reality control. I'll admit, as occultists, we might reasonably be accused of dilettantism. We're dabblers. Throw it at the wall and see what sticks. These days we're on a curse tablet kick. *Defixiones,* Walter. Are you hip? It's an ancient Greek thing." He set his eyes on the trays. "The sand and water, full of the city's refuse, bind these tablets to our target. Tonight we'll inscribe them with death curses for the metropolis, for capital, for modernity." He cracked his neck. "And you can help. I need guys like you. On the inside. You know, I like these people," he said, looking around the cabin, "but they're freaks. We need more straight-world double agents. Hedge funders, private equity, big tech. You guys are closest to the demon. You're the ones making it happen. The more money you pull out of your hats, the closer we all get. Wealth inequality, ecological collapse, infrastructure decay, political instability. The sort of thing that happened to your wife." He looked into my eyes and shrugged. "All that kind of shit."

I felt a hand on my side. Aggie. She smiled. Then she shot through my jacket and pulled out the painting. Green dabs for blossoming trees, pale sky. "Oh, wow," Lucca said. "Yes, yes! That's a *great* fucking binding agent. Treacly, insipid. An entirely uncritical representation. Whoever painted that must be a total fucking zombie. Hey, you're all right, Walter." He laughed, grabbed my thigh and squeezed.

When Aggie broke the frame over her knee, tears stung my eyes. She tore loose the canvas, used a razor to cut it away from the backing, and then sliced it into strips. They were passed around and folded into the mixtures. Someone gave one to me, cut from the painting's center—a portion of the large tree in our neighbor's yard, half of the Williamsburg Bank Building, its high tower split unevenly by Aggie's razor—but I didn't know what to do with it; I couldn't drop it into that churning muck.

"All right," said Lucca, "let's get some essence of extraction capitalist into these tablets." The others put down their tools and made toward me. I pushed up onto the balls of my feet, squirmed against the wall. Their eyes were empty in the weird light and for one second I thought maybe they'd kill me. "Get him, my pretties," muttered Lucca, rubbing his left eye with the heel of his hand. "Get his—what? Hair, I guess." He grabbed my wrist, examined my cuticles. "And his toenails, maybe. They're too short to clip, on his fingers. What're your toenails like, Walter?" Aggie held me by the shoulders while Carla crouched and pulled my flip-flops off.

When it was over, Lucca sighed. "What say we have a drink while these things set, huh? Here, give some to him." A bottle fell into my lap. "Christ, Walter," he said as I drank, "you're going to get us all fucking sick, man. Oh well. Hurry up, give it here." Carla came and sat on his lap, kissed his ear, and Aggie put her head on my shoulder. I wanted then to get as drunk as I possibly could, and as I did so I moved through the ship like nothing, a wisp. I pitched up onto the deck, fell into the night air and saw the city, white-gold now, helicopters hanging among the towers as if on wires. I pissed into the water, humming "Take On Me," and it struck me then that I could force my voice out, if I wanted. I took a breath and made to whoop. The sound tore from my throat, and I doubled over in agony. Tilly nudged her head under my arm and cozied in. I laughed; suddenly I loved her. After the night turned cold, I found Aggie with Sim in the prow. He hissed at her, "Where the fuck do you get off? How do you think it makes me feel?" She turned to me, her face interrupting a slick of light across the water behind her. "Walter, not now." As I stumbled off, I heard her say, "I don't know, Sim. He reminds me of my dad. Anyway, that's what taking a break *is*—it's a *break*, you know?" Boats kept arriving, tying up to the *Weasel*. The deck grew crowded. Someone asked if I'd seen Hector: "He's our TA." A pack of kids—I might have taken them for Bea's age. Later I found Aggie with Sim in the hold, the two of them half undressed atop a pile of life vests.

And later again I became aware of Lucca's voice, incanting at the piercing top of its register. Everything was tilting and shadowed. He was in the prow, under a hanging spotlight. The crowd formed a semicircle before him, and beyond, across the water, the skyline glimmered. In a cloak, with a smoking gold censer, he leapt rhythmically, the censer flying on its chain into the air after him, floating an instant before falling back down. He was conducting a sort of mass.

"Bind and constrict the city!" he shrieked. "Darken its towers—lies built upon lies, lies multiplied by lies!" He pointed to the skyline. "Adored by all but by us abhorred, be thou accursed, be thou annihilated, be thou abolished!" From the crowd, a muttered *Amen*. I pushed my way up. There with Lucca were the tablets, propped on easels in the circle of light, attended by Aggie, Hector, others, all of them now in white gowns. With nails, they etched blunt phrases into the wet concrete. The ship teemed with all sorts, young, old, some costumed, leather and eyeliner, cloaks, capes. The crowd was solemn in one instant, antic the next. At midship, a DJ was setting up.

All at once, I noticed that I'd staggered through the crowd and into the light. Lucca stopped his incanting, let his shoulders fall, gestured at me with an open hand. "Walter, ladies and gentlemen." They all laughed. Lucca turned to Aggie. "Hey, Aggie, I think this guy is like blacked out."

"*Wal*ter," she hissed, her iron nail clattering to the deck as she grabbed for my arm.

I pulled away, braced against the brass rail. The crowd murmured and jeered, some giggling, others booing. An empty beer can skipped off my shoulder, sailing behind me into the night.

I turned to watch it go, saw the skyline, and thought: That's where Bea is.

Maybe she'd gone to the roof and found my phone in the gardening chest. On the screen she'd have seen both her own messages and missed calls from her grandfather. Of course she'd dwell on the possibility I was hurt, or worse. She knew how simple it was for someone to leave home and never return. Perhaps she'd lit the way back to her room with her phone, and, in bed, spoken in soft tones to her mother. I knew she did so. With my ear to the door, I'd heard her.

The DJ began his set. Costumed people in the shifting light, the dark and droning music—it was like a cartoon hell. What sort of party was this? I felt confused, looking at the tablets. There were pieces of me inside them. Nora, too. I thought about what Lucca wanted, or said he did, and imagined, like in a time-lapse, all the buildings on the skyline crumbling, splitting vertically, big halves of office towers sliding down in succeeding avalanches, until it was just a great nothing, collapsed into a frozen crater ringed by tundra. The ice was too dull to sparkle and nothing moved. It was silent and still, absent me, absent my daughter and her mother and all of us wrapped so madly up in life.

I wanted to go home.

Tilly was there in the aft, head resting on her paws like a sleeping sphinx. A kindred spirit, another voiceless attendant to these weird proceedings, alone, probably hungry—had anyone fed her? She stood, stretched, yawned, raised one white paw to me. As I reached to take it, she hopped into my arms, her legs slipping out of my grip and then scratching back up. I leaned over the ship's railing, lowered her down, dropped her into the same graying canoe that had delivered us to the *Weasel,* now one of many small vessels assembled in the waters there. She barked up at me. I swung my legs over and clattered in behind her, then stood to untie us.

As I worked my fingers through the rope, my body buckled and I coughed, sputtered, and vomited down the side of the ship, into the water and the bottom of the canoe, onto my feet. I gasped and moaned, expelling it all. And when I'd finished, I looked up to see someone above me there on the deck. My eyes were level with the pointed toes of his shoes. He wore a black leather bodysuit with a long cape and his face was painted white. One hand on the railing, he looked down into my eyes. It took a long moment for me to understand that it was Denton Whitwell.

"Let me help you, Walter," he said and untied us. "That cleat's a little loose, and I don't want you to pull it out." He passed the rope to me and smiled. "This is my boat, you understand."

I took up the oar and pushed off into the tide. The canoe rocked slowly out and away.

I stared at him, receding. His smile was untroubled, collegial. "Safe travels," he said. "I'm sorry we didn't get to chat. Glad that you're up and about, though. We missed you this week." He shrugged. "I'll hope to see you around the club, at any rate. Or back here on the *Weasel*, with Lucca. As you prefer."

Now we were ten yards out. I took up the oars.

"Oh," he said, "please don't worry about tonight. We've all had a bit too much, from time to time. I won't breathe a word to Len." Denton waved. A big, sweeping gesture, like from atop a parade float.

I turned toward the shore.

Behind me, he called out, "And my regards to Beatrice!"

## 13

First light bloomed in the clouds and in the branches. I didn't know the way through the woods, but Tilly did, and when a train rumbled along the tracks, going back the way we'd come—a garbage train, matching Redbirds on either end—we hopped on together.

I curled myself around her on the hard bench, buried my face in her curls.

I pretended she was Nora. I told her that I couldn't keep on by myself.

You have to, she said.

I said, I know. I know. I can't.

She said, You have to.

## 14

Richie Dee was on the platform when we disembarked, doing Billy Joel, "Tell Her About It." He sang delicately, fingerpicking; he'd made it a folk song. The scattered few waiting turned to see Tilly and me. We made an odd sight, tumbling all disheveled from the garbage train. For the first time, I noticed that I'd lost a flip-flop. Richie nodded at me as we passed. From then on, when I saw him, I always gave him a buck or two.

Under the Mesa's awning, Tilly and I made our farewell. I knelt to her; she licked my face. I felt she was owed something—a treat?—but of course I had nothing, and, patting my thighs, I discovered that my wallet too had, at some point in the whole awful thing, gone missing. Those shallow sweatpants pockets. All I had was my house key, that realtor's card, and—impossibly, it seemed, as my fingers brushed over it—that strip of Nora's painting. But had I in fact brought the wallet? I tried to think. I'd look when I got home, and if it weren't there, I'd call Chase and the DMV and the MTA about issuing new cards. I'd email Dave, who took care of the badges we used to swipe through the turnstiles in the copper-colored lobby on Park Avenue. It was all replaceable.

The thing to do, I supposed, was to go straight to Bea's room, wake her, try and explain. I entered the house quietly, hung my jacket on the hook beside her backpack. Then I went to the bathroom to wash my face with scalding water. And I started laughing, looking at myself in the mirror, and laughed until tears came down my cheeks, and I buried my face in the crook of my arm, doubled over, resting on the sink basin with the water still running and steaming the glass.

I walked down the stairs to Bea's room and opened her door. But her bed was primly made, untouched since the previous morning. The room felt cold. I was terrified. Something awful might have happened. Bea could have been all over the news that morning and I wouldn't know. I ran to the roof for my phone, then collapsed out of breath into one of the deck chairs to read my texts. She had sent several, and she'd called. The last text said that, because she didn't know where I was, she was going to a friend's. From Len I had nothing at all.

I was lying on the couch when I heard the front door. Bea, in dark jeans and a knit cap, came and sat across from me in the floral chair. She was drained of color, her eyes were watery. I half suspected that she'd vomited not long before entering.

I whispered, "You look like shit."

"Ditto," she said.

I coughed; it was agony. "Were you somewhere safe?"

"Sharon Liptak's."

"Sharon Liptak's," I repeated. The grandfather clock ticked. I said, "Parents?"

But Bea only asked, "What about you?"

"Me?"

"Were you somewhere safe?"

My eyes throbbed. "I was," I began, and then found myself unsure how to continue. What should I tell her? Where *had* I been? "I was on a boat. I was on a boat with Poppy's friend. Denton Whitwell." I swallowed. "It was a weird night. I'm sorry."

She said, "Poppy needs you to call him."

On Monday, I knew, Len would fill me in on what I'd missed the week before. I'd learn how we were to put Denton's counsel into practice over the coming months. Len would be excited, of course: We'd stand to make a killing. And before long, I would run into Denton again. Somewhere on the Upper East Side. In a restaurant, or at the club, or maybe just on the street. His toad's head would sink into his neck as he grinned; he'd take my wrist and pull me close.

"Let's call in sick," I said to Bea. "We both need it."

"It's Saturday."

"Then we won't call anyone, we'll just be sick." I realized then that I hadn't eaten since before I could remember. "I want pancakes," I said. "Order us pancakes. Would you? And eggs and sausage. And cheeseburgers. A pizza, ice cream, cake, whatever, do five different restaurants if you want."

I asked Bea to put something on to watch, and she chose old episodes of *Friends*. A world of distraction—I was glad she could have this; I felt thankful to the people who made things like it. We watched from separate perches. I had to reach far back to imagine when she would have lain atop me, a little thing, arms thrown back around my neck. We ate extravagantly. And afterward, when the show had lulled me half to sleep, I dreamed, or sort of imagined, that Nora was there with us. Whole and sound. I took her hand in mine, raised it to my lips, and kissed her once on each knuckle.

"Hey," I said to Bea when I woke, turning my head to see her, "I'm sorry. Really."

"I know," she said, but she didn't move her eyes from the screen. And I felt too sick to explain that I was sorry not just for last night, but for all of it—all the work incumbent upon her, upon anyone, of assembling a universe in which to live, from scratch and anew, when that work is so hard.

Each time an episode ended a new one began, and as I dozed, the laugh track was in my dreams—people laughing and clapping, whistling and hooting, for what might have been forever.

I woke again and the television was off. The light had deepened.

"I'm getting up really soon," I said, stretching and rubbing my eyes. "I promise."

But Bea was curled up, her head on the chair's armrest, fast asleep.

## GOLF CART

Up through the open window came the sound of small tires on gravel. Twice he punched the horn. I stood from the desk, crossed the room, leaned over the sill to see him—my older brother—looking up from behind the wheel of the golf cart.

Through the screen, I called down, "Explain yourself."

"Busy night, man. Need help."

Crickets, cicadas, fireflies, the tumult of mid-Atlantic deep summer, near midnight.

I yawned and rolled my neck. "Describe it, then."

"All kinds of incursions onto the property. A pickup truck was sitting in front of the gate. Now it's going up and down Hedgewood Road. The neighbors are having what sounds like a party. And there was something strange in the Far Pasture. Some kind of disturbance. The night's thick, man. My eyes are fucked. I don't know what it was."

I glanced over my shoulder. A new, unfinished piece of pixel art glowed on the laptop's display. "Yeah, well," I said, "I'm working now. Anyway, I still haven't packed." My flight to Michigan was at six in the morning. I'd arranged for a car at four. He knew perfectly well that I didn't have time for another one of his expeditions. "Look, I can't deal with this. Not tonight. I'm sorry."

But he shook his head, arms crossed atop the steering wheel, then turned his gaze toward the fields. He was one year from thirty, five years my elder. Since December, when I'd moved back East, the two of us had shared a long, homebound season together. All our little dramas were worn to nearly nothing. He knew I'd come.

Outside, the night air felt warm and cool both. My brother sat in the golf cart, glasses dangling from his mouth, phone pressed absurdly near to one squinting eye. He had inherited his abysmal eyesight from our father, who now, in his midsixties, had serious trouble with road signs and even facial expressions in low light. But my brother was still young. And he had a way of making any ailment or weakness seem principled, as if he didn't avoid tree nuts for his allergies or bright sun for his delicate complexion but as a matter of taste. He was tall and very thin, his shaggy hair just slightly strawberry-toned. Physically, his most angular features defined him—sharp nose and chin, pronounced Adam's apple, knees that pointed whenever he bent his spindly frame into some too-small space, as just then, in the golf cart. He wore his tattered old Animal Collective shirt under a button-down, left open. I slid onto the cream-toned vinyl beside him and placed, briefly, an arm across his shoulders. He nodded. Then, after that weightless instant between the click of the pedal and the cart's cute whinnying thrust, we were off.

It was a good golf cart, a classic white Club Car, though at fifteen it was near in age to Henrietta, our chocolate Lab—she was blind herself, poor thing, and incontinent. The golf cart wasn't quite so badly off, though it did strain going up hills, and the tires always sounded flat, and it wouldn't hold its charge. Of course, it was hard to say whether those impressions were subjectively colored. Like the fatigue listed as a side effect of our father's chemotherapy pills: How to be sure, he'd wonder aloud, as to the *source* of one's fatigue? The question seemed to haunt him.

I said, "Tell me about the disturbance."

"Disturbanc*es*," my brother snapped. "Multiple." We bounced over a dip in the pavement, front wheels then back. "We'll need a full sweep of the property. Head to the Far Pasture first, I'd say. From there we can keep an eye on the road for that pickup truck. Now, in terms of weaponry, what do you prefer?"

I looked over my shoulder to see what lay in the bed. "Seven iron."

"Fine. Then I'll take the rifle." An antique: our grandfather's slender .22.

I yawned, stretched both arms high, and resettled. We made the driveway's steepest ascent, up from the old guesthouse we called the Lodge, where I'd been staying, and on toward what we called the Cottage, where my brother lived, before climbing to the Main House, our father's, in which we'd grown up. We made the hill's peak, as slow as a roller coaster, and then revealed below us were the hundred acres of bare gentle hills, shady groves, and brook-laced meadows of the family property we called the Farm.

"My God," he whispered, reverent, "it is straight fucking Hyrule out here tonight."

Silver waving grass, the motor's quiet hum.

The moon was low, enormous, the color of an old flashlight under a sheet, and each time I glanced back it looked higher. In fact, it did seem to bowl up the sky just like—he was precisely right—the moon in a *Zelda* game. Really, all the night's beauty was so garish I could have mistaken it for digital. I'd been too long in the screen realm, holed up in the Lodge, at work on my new pixel-art series. My hope was to debut a few pieces that week in East Lansing, at Michigan State's Digital Humanities Center, where I'd been invited for something called the Emerging Formats Conference. I'd had to pay my own airfare and all of that—to be perfectly clear, when it came to pixel art, I was a hobbyist. But earlier that year, my debut series, *July '95*, had garnered some notice on Tumblr and Twitter. Several artists I admired had followed my accounts, or even shared my work. And now a handful of those would be at

Michigan State. I couldn't draw freehand, had no training; I didn't imagine a real future for myself as an artist. And I knew the kind of affair the Emerging Formats Conference would be: urn coffee in an obscure classroom, unclaimed name-tag lanyards, projector malfunctions. But I wouldn't have missed it. Pixels made sense to me. I liked the way you could focus for hours, laying them like beads, fine-tuning the light, the shading, absorbed in the minutiae of a piece until dawn. And I had a knack for the scene's dominant aesthetic. The most perfect GIF of all time, in my opinion, had been posted in 2016 by an anonymous Japanese artist: quiet neon alleyway, late night, a vending machine's backlit display softly flickering. All the best work was like that—gorgeous and forlorn, animated with the barest traces of movement. *July '95* was my own modest contribution to the genre. The series concerned the suburban American commerce of my boyhood: Pizza Hut, CompUSA, Borders Books and Music, the storefronts rendered in the style of old 16-bit games, depicted at some remove from near-empty parking lots. Late afternoons, pale dusks. I had a good eye.

As we thumped past the end of the pavement and onto the grass, my brother flicked off the headlights. I didn't worry; he'd driven this way countless nights and never missed a trick. He reached into the cupholder to raise the volume on his phone, and from the speaker clipped to the dash came a rolling clatter of drums, thick spidering bass, and that lead guitar I'd know anywhere, a delicate ornamentation, like tinsel.

I asked, "Veneta, '72?"

"No. Berkeley, three nights earlier. This is an all-time great version of 'Dark Star.' Summer 1972 through the hiatus in '74: the Grateful Dead's pinnacle. Now, I want you to listen," he said, raising the volume again, "thinking not only about the 'Dark Star' jam itself but the way that, after spooling out for thirty fucking minutes, okay, to the brink and back, multiple times, the band will slip with elegance and grace and heart and wisdom and humility and winking humor, even, out of that sprawling psychedelic morass and straight into, of all things, a cover of Marty Robbins's 'El Paso.'" At the end of the sentence his voice buckled—slightly, only I would have heard it—and I saw his eyes glisten. The depth of his feeling was a kind of genius. It was part of what I loved so much in him. "The vision," he said, "the commingling of forms, the beating heart of American creativity . . ."

"Utterly fucked," I agreed. "But doesn't this one go into 'Morning Dew'?"

He shook his head. "'El Paso.'"

We swished down the hill on a stripe cut through the high grass, a trail crisscrossing the entire property—it ran from the end of the pavement and past the goat pen to the Far Pasture, then over the brook to the East Clearing, through the woods to the Upper Fields, and back. May through September, Ignacio and his son came once a week to mow the trail. On either side of it now the grass was chest-high, impassable, full of grasshoppers and ticks. My brother was fanatical on the subject of ticks. When we were young, our mother had spent a long year suffering from Lyme disease, undiagnosed and untreated. Now my brother would lecture me if I didn't hang my socks and jeans on the outside line after walking in the fields. And whenever I found a tick crawling under my sleeve or collar or, God forbid, burrowed into my skin, he'd go on and on, exasperated and amazed, about the near-calamity I had just barely escaped through sheer dumb luck.

Now we reached top speed with the goat pen just ahead. At the sound of our approach, the goats came trotting from the goat house and up to the edge of their pen— Lester, Doc, and Earl, named by our father for bluegrass greats.

My brother saluted as we passed. "At ease, boys."

I should explain that the goats were an affectation. They served no end, I mean, besides aesthetics. Calling our property the Farm was an affectation, too. It *had* been one, long ago—there was an old barn with milking stalls, and the low-slung shed where we stacked our firewood was once a chicken coop. But there had been no agriculture in the area for a hundred years. We didn't live in the country. We were ten miles from downtown Wilmington, Delaware, twenty-five from Philadelphia, and mere minutes from the dazzling hell of big-box highway commerce on Route 202. Rambling properties like ours were by then quite rare—they'd been sold off and subdivided, mainly, the green hills leveled and dozens of new houses slapped up. We were members of a small group of holdouts along Hedgewood Road, an old country lane with no lights or stop signs. It was one of the area's last unspoiled tracts. Hedgewood terminated at either end in well-trafficked corridors, but in between, it wound past several large estates, the houses all hidden from the road by hills and thick forest. Tucker Foote was our neighbor through the woods. His mansion, a true historic marvel, had a working hydroelectric dam designed by Edison and a family library that required a full-time archivist. Tuck had been like an uncle to us, growing up, though his blood ran bluer than ours. He was a du Pont. And so were we, although farther out along the family tree. I could never keep all the connections straight. My brother knew those things. And he knew which beams in our Main House were original eighteenth century, and the details of the midtwenties restoration by R. Brognard Okie, the colonial revivalist, and all the most unusual specimens in the arboretum down by the pond, now gone wild, though overseen in its glory days by Jan Bernhauser, the Winterthur horticulturalist. It was a sort of vocation for my brother: lover and keeper of the Farm.

"Here," he said as we rolled into the Far Pasture, a wide space jeweled at its center with one tight-packed oak grove. He stopped the cart, motioned vaguely toward the high grass. "Look—there—do you see anything? Earlier there were strange rustlings. A sense of presence."

"No," I said, settling back. "But I believe you."

He turned the music down. I watched the moon through my eyelids. I was still a little high.

He whispered, "Hear that?"

I said nothing. He waved his hand frantically at me and shushed.

The grass before us roiled with the imperfections of my night vision: flashes, colors.

But then, yes, something moved. I did see it. There was something in the fields. Crouching, maybe. I thought I saw hunched shoulders. A ducked head. Or two, even.

My blood quickened. I sat up. "You were right."

"Do you think it's the neighbors?" He raised the rifle to his shoulder.

"Careful with that thing," I said. "It's not loaded, is it?"

"Okay," he whispered, "get ready. Switch on the lights."

I did. Like a chip shot falling short, the golf cart's headlights arced out and then drooped into the grass before us. But in their farthest reaches I saw eyes. Four of them, buttery and cool. The eyes were pointed at us, and we were pointed at the eyes. My brother's body tensed around the gun; I gripped the seven iron just under its head and held my breath. Then two pale shapes rose above the stalks: a broad-chested buck, its left antler broken and jagged in the moonlight, and a lissome doe. For one solemn instant they appraised us, coats sheening. Then they turned and pranced down the hill.

He lowered the rifle and exhaled. "Well," he said, "the Far Pasture is secure."

"Turn it back up," I said, and he did. The Dead, half a century earlier, had abandoned their harmonic center, playing raucous and angular now. They were getting out there. I liked the Grateful Dead's music because you could get lost in it. Same reason I liked pixel art: Each GIF was a little world. And now the impulse toward a new piece gathered in my mind. Purple sky, big moon, long view of the grass and the deer's four irradiated eyes. Yes. A thrill ran up my spine. It had come to me, unbidden and whole, and I could see it, exactly as it would be—in fact, the scene was so perfect that it seemed just to have *been* pixel art, already, as I had witnessed it. All summer, that'd been happening. Through my work I was giving instruction to my eye. Inflecting my own lived reality. My practice was changing how I saw.

Suddenly, I wanted to explain all this to my brother. But he was peering so intently into the night.

"That fucking pickup truck again," he muttered.

Way down the hill and through the trees, headlights rolled north on Hedgewood Road.

"How can you tell? How do you know it's a pickup?" I was thinking of his eyes.

He scowled at me. "The way it's *moving,* man. This is what I've been doing. Do you understand? While you sit in the Lodge making your clip art or whatever it is. Look how slowly they're driving. They've got no legitimate business here, not at this hour. What day is it? Isn't it Saturday?" He clucked his tongue. "Kids. Bad, bad naughty ones. Joyriders. Looking for trouble. And capable of violence."

It was hard to tell when he was joking. He always was, sort of.

But it was true that, late at night, stoned kids from Wilmington and the suburbs did come carousing out along Hedgewood Road. For as long as I could remember, it had been a problem. Hedgewood's shoulders were littered with butts and cans most Monday mornings, and now and then we'd find the meadow at the southern tip of the Farm, where for years a length of fence had been down, slashed with muddy tire tracks. I'd never quite understood it—there was nothing to see on Hedgewood, just the handful of gated driveways. But the place had long been the subject of local folklore. The road lent itself to that, I suppose, with its crooked trees, one-lane bridge, and thick surrounding woods. Back in school, kids would ask us whether it was true that Satanists performed occult rituals around Hedgewood. There were stories of weird lights back in the trees. And of course there was the legend about the Foote mansion. Even our father recalled hearing that one as a boy. Tuck's place was said to have been haunted by all the inbred, stillborn du Pont babies supposedly buried on its grounds.

Half to himself, my brother said, "If we zip back now we could head them off at the gate."

I looked at him, tried to read his expression.

But then he made a small grunt of displeasure, way down in his throat. "No. Bad math. We'd never make it. Let's change tack."

And he threw the golf cart into reverse, then sent us whirring back into motion, climbing up and through a narrow band of trees, out to the Upper Fields, where the air was cooler and hung with the faintest suggestion of dew. My eyes were closed, still visualizing the deer, mentally assembling pixels. I would start on the piece as soon as I got back to the Lodge. It felt urgent. I'd set aside my other works in progress. They were uninspired, anyway—just retreads of *July '95*. For weeks that suspicion had nagged me, and now the vision of the deer had confirmed it. The best of my new pieces was *Mall Fountain*. Too obvious, too derivative. But the buck's broken antler, the absence of light. There was something there.

My brother parked the golf cart near the edge of our property, where a small grove of trees separated us from the neighbors. To say "the neighbors" was sufficient; there were no others so closely adjoining us. Their house, of a characterless new construction, was at the end of a cul-de-sac in Belle Vista, the only large development abutting our property. It went up when I was in high school. There was no entrance to Belle Vista on Hedgewood; I'd never seen the neighbors up close. But their ATVs left tracks across our Upper Fields, they spattered our trees with paintballs, the goats ate the cardboard that rained down from their janky fireworks. Regular sportsmen, our father joked. Now there were lights through the trees, and we could hear music from their back deck: pop-country of the newest stripe, dense with production and auto-tuned vocals.

"What are they doing up so late?" my brother said. "I don't like it."

As if to answer his question, a small firework whistled drunkenly up from their yard and burst above us, cherry-red.

Pixel art, I thought.

Half to himself, my brother said, "We need a fence up here. The vulnerability is real."

For a long moment, we listened to the distant music. The fireflies looked as big as golf balls.

I was thinking over the details of my flight—the air-freshened interior of the car that would pick me up in the dark, the startling abruptness with which I'd find myself with scores of others in the security line. I took my phone from my pocket to see if the departure was still on time.

He tolerated it briefly. Then he said, "Put that thing away. I don't trust you to have the permissions set right. It's going to record our conversation and send it off to an overseas server to be strip-mined for emotional surplus data."

I sighed, pocketing the phone. "I don't believe that. Anyway, what are we supposed to be looking at here? I'd say the Upper Pasture is pretty secure, too."

"Let me tell you what your problem is," he said, shifting the gun on his lap. "You've got no imagination. You don't appreciate how bad things are out there. There's nothing good coming for us. Do you understand that? Think how much the neighbors must hate us. Wouldn't you, if you were them? They've got all the reason in the world. What you're observing here is an uneasy peace. When the shit hits the fan, this is the kind of place people will go. They'll be roaming in packs. Looking for potable water." He sat back, crossed his right leg over his left. "Zero imagination. I love you, but it's true. Everything's going to shit. Look at these trees, even." He waved his hand. "Full of holes from the lantern flies. And then of course there's Dad's health. Dad's in really bad shape, you know. He's practically at death's door."

He knew it bothered me when he said that. Our father was a gentle man, long-legged, with a slight hunch, one wandering eye, always smiling inscrutably. He'd retired early and been sustained thereafter by a passion for birding, which had led him to close involvement in local conservation efforts. Now that my brother and I were both living at home, we had dinner with our father about once a week. He'd invite us to the Main House by text, two or three days in advance, and the hour we'd spend at his table always felt long. My brother and I had lived our lives without really getting to know our father very well. Maybe that's why I felt such affection for him. I'd always suspected that if Dad had been born later, his halting mannerisms and trouble with crowds might have been given a name—something clinical. When my brother and I were young, he'd step into a room we occupied, hands in his pockets, make an obscure remark in his nasal, high-pitched voice—*It's the Pep Boys,* for example, *Manny and Moe, but no Jack*—and then turn, like a soldier, and be gone.

"Dad is not at death's door," I said. "It's an irresponsible statement."

"So, what, then—ten more years? Fifteen?"

"He's in remission."

"Yes, and the treatment he's receiving didn't exist a decade ago. That's almost the same as it not existing now.

When you barely escape a horror, the horror inflects the escape. I love you, brother, but I'm telling you—it's going to be you and me. You'd better get ready. Best-case scenario, when Dad gets too old to walk up the stairs, he'll sell this place. We'll need to strike out on our own. And, forgive me, but we all saw how that went when you tried it."

He was needling, now. Being cruel.

Out of college, I took a job with Spotify and moved to Brooklyn. My brother hadn't approved—I was part of the surveillance capitalist industrial complex, debasing myself, and in the process helping to urge on, more or less, the apocalypse. In any case, the fit was poor. I started having panic attacks again, on the subway. That prompted a change in my medication, and we couldn't get it dialed in. My insomnia came back. The work went badly and the job didn't last. I left the city, went out to our house in Jackson Hole, took a string of remote programming gigs. But when I came home to the Farm for Christmas, I couldn't see any real reason to go West again. The Lodge was just sitting there. I didn't know what to do next. I had no plans. All I had was my pixel art. Still, when my brother spoke that way to me, retorts sprang to mind. He'd never gone anywhere at all, never had a real job or a relationship. He was only an assistant tennis coach at our old high school, and occasionally a substitute teacher. He saw less and less of the few friends he had. He sat in the Cottage, smoking cannabis resin, ordering groceries for delivery, sometimes walking up the hill to hit golf balls beside the barn. But no matter how he tried to wound me, I could never level those things at him.

He turned the golf cart around and set us back onto the path. The grass was highest in the Upper Fields, the trail shaggiest. We moved slowly. At the property's southern end, the trail veered right to make a steep descent through a band of thick forest. The moon was higher now, so everything was bluer, and the Dead had moseyed into pleasant territory—a noncommittal groove, wooden-soldier bass, the gauzy, modal inversions of the rhythm guitar.

Below us, on Hedgewood, slow-moving headlights painted the trees. I guessed it was the pickup, the same one we'd seen before. But this time, my brother let it pass unremarked. It was late, our ride nearly over. And because he'd sowed the ground for it with his dig at me, I knew he would broach the real topic at hand, as sooner or later he always did.

He turned the music up and said, "When Jerry Garcia was four years old, he watched his father drown in a river in Humboldt County. They'd gone for a day of fly-fishing. See, you have something like *that* in your personal history, in your makeup, and it spurs you to do the thing you need to do. It's a kind of permission. And after that, you—"

I'd heard him say it before, so I finished his thought: "You don't worry about petty social or material concerns. You've peeked around the stage curtain and seen that void out where the seats were meant to be. You're liberated, then."

He turned to me. He seemed pleased. "Bless him. Bless our Saint Jerry."

"It is right to give him thanks and praise," I muttered.

"Well," he said, "but that's exactly right. You're thrown off the grid by tragedy. You become one of life's cowboys. We had none of that."

"We had the divorce."

He shook his head. "The divorce doesn't count. I'm telling you, I've given this a lot of thought. It's not in the cards for us. Greatness. Or basic competence, even. Because of this." His gesture swept up everything around us.

The golf cart rolled out of the trees and into the open air. We followed the trail down the grassy hill, along a series of wide switchbacks. Nestled in its dark hollow at the bottom of the hill was the Lodge. The soft light visible through the second-floor window was my laptop's display. We bounced up onto the pavement. He stopped beside the front door and depressed the golf cart's parking brake.

We sat awhile.

Then I said, "But with some self-awareness, you *could* do something. You could get something done. Something worthwhile. I know that you could." I said it to him, and I meant it. But I was also thinking of myself.

The music played. A breeze moved in the pines.

He sighed. "None of this makes sense, anyway. Look at this." Helplessly, he indicated the trees, the grass, the night sky. "What the fuck *is* it? I don't know what's going on here, but it's not what it looks like. It can't be. The universe must be an illusion, somehow. A hologram, or—I don't know what you'd call it. But any idiot can see things aren't on the level. There's no way life is real."

I heard something strange, from way off in the distance. It was some kind of whirring.

"What's that?" I asked.

The sound stopped, then started again, the pitch rising and falling. A metallic bleat.

"Oh my God," he said. He looked at me, amazed and incensed. "It's doughnuts. It's that pickup, those fucking animals—they're doing *doughnuts* in our meadow."

And before I could protest, he gunned it, sending the golf cart as fast as it could go—not so very fast; it had a built-in limiter—up the long hill once more, past the Cottage, then to the Main House, and now he veered left, straight down the driveway, past the Pond and the Arboretum, racing toward Hedgewood Road. Bent hard over the wheel, rifle between his knees, he drove right up to the gate, which gleamed like a set of teeth in the moonlight, and stopped where he knew we'd trip the motion sensors. The gate began to whine open, and the noise from the meadow was much louder now, much closer to us— engine revving, mud spattering, dull thudding bass.

The night air beat in my ears; I felt panicky. "Look," I said, "what do you want to do? You want to, like, confront them? Let's just get out of here." I'd ridden with him plenty of nights, but we'd never done anything like this.

Now the gate was wide open. We stared out into nothing.

As the crow flies, the pickup was less than a hundred

yards from us, but that meadow, the one with the broken fence, lay beyond a dense thicket of thorns and brambles. It was barely possible to walk through it, let alone drive the golf cart. And so I knew what my brother was thinking. Having torn up our grass, they wouldn't hang around; in just another minute or two they'd look to make their escape. And the quickest way out of there and back to civilization was to turn right, north, onto Hedgewood—straight toward us, where we sat parked in the golf cart at the mouth of the driveway. What's more, because our driveway began at a sharp westward crook in the road, the pickup would approach us directly. For several seconds as they fled, their headlights would be dead on us.

Out in the meadow, tires wailed. My brother raised the rifle, peered down the barrel.

"Hey," I said. "Put that thing down."

The darkness before us was thicker and more alive with every second. We listened as the truck's engine stalled, coughed, then revved clean, and the night was quiet enough that I could hear their tires breeze out onto the pavement. Beyond the crook in Hedgewood Road, through the trees, I saw their headlights.

"Hey," I said again.

He settled the rifle's butt into his shoulder.

"What are you doing? You're not—you wouldn't—are you going to shoot them?"

He glared over the bolt, astonished. "No, I'm not going to shoot them. You think I would *shoot* them?"

The engine roared. They were approaching the crook.

He snapped back to attention. "This is it."

And the lights were on us.

For one instant—they must have been taking stock—the pickup braked. I couldn't see the truck then; I could only see its high beams. But I knew what they saw: the open gate, the golf cart, my brother and me, the seven iron, and the barrel of that rifle. Then they floored it. The truck shot toward us, it was twenty yards out, and then ten; it hit the crook in the road and swerved hard to our right. A mud-spattered white Dodge, its windows tinted, moving in a lurid halo cast by neon-lit rocker panels. Heavy bass sawed through a subwoofer. For one instant, it was so close that I almost could have touched it with the seven iron.

Then, just as the lights slid off us, when the truck was poised to slingshot past the crook and north up Hedgewood, something leapt from the roadside. A blurred shape, suspended for an instant in the truck's headlights. It smashed into the grille. The truck's brakes locked; we saw its back end jump. Their music stopped. Then everything was still.

When I uncovered my face, I saw that it was the buck. The same one: broken left antler, eyes wide and pointed at us. The buck's body was now under the truck, but the right antler had jammed into the grille and wedged there, so that its head and broken neck interrupted the right headlight beam. I looked for the doe and found her half-lit on the shoulder. She made three confused revolutions and crashed off through the trees.

The minutes that followed were tense and strange. Doors opened on both sides of the truck, and out stepped three boys. They couldn't have been more than seventeen. There was a tall, scrawny one, a flat-brimmed hat set askew on his narrow head. There was a fat, shaggy one, wearing a brass padlock as a necklace. And then there was the driver, imposingly built, with heavy arms and strong shoulders. All white. And red-faced, and young. Together, they worked with grim concentration to free the buck from the grille. They had to twist its head. They took the buck by the neck and pulled and shook it, negotiating quietly with one another, more than once counting to three in whispers before an effort. My brother sat silent and unflinching, breathing loudly but evenly. The one in the hat kept looking back at us. It felt like an eternity.

Then with a wrenching sound, the buck fell loose. The driver and the one with the padlock each took a hind leg and dragged it to the far side of the road. They swung it around by the legs so that it was mostly off the pavement. The one with the hat said something, and the driver nodded, knelt down, pressed both hands into the buck's side, and rolled it into the ferns and dead leaves. The boys wiped their hands on their jeans, mopped their brows with their forearms. They climbed back into the truck. And before he closed his door, the driver called out to us: "Fucking psychos."

They drove north along Hedgewood, very slowly. My brother lowered the rifle.

The Dead had collapsed into an ambient territory. No

drums, long spaces between notes, flashes of total silence. At length, they swam up out of "Dark Star" and into "Morning Dew."

I was shivering, staring at the blood on the road.

My brother put the golf cart into reverse. It beeped as we made a three-point turn. "You were right," he muttered. "It's not 'El Paso.'" The gate closed behind us, and then we began the labored ascent back toward the Main House.

My brother drove down to the Lodge and parked outside the front door, leaned back, and exhaled. "Well," he said. "They won't be back. That's for sure." But he said it strangely.

Behind us, the bullfrog who lived at the Pond began to croak. I was searching for something to say and couldn't find it. A short while passed.

Then he said, "I've been having such trouble sleeping. To be honest, I'm dreading being alone in bed. When I can't sleep, I have this fantasy that I use. Have I ever told you about this? No, I guess I've never told anyone. I visualize myself out in the fields. A flying saucer slips from behind a cloud and lifts me up. It's warm and pleasant inside the saucer, and I can direct it with my mind. It can fly anywhere in the universe. Down to the ocean floor, or into a cave on a far-off planet. And the saucer emanates this force, or power, that keeps me safe from any threat. What I mean by that is, say I shoot unwittingly into an asteroid belt. The saucer knows how to steer me. It's invisible to any hostile energy, no matter how unimaginable. I can go wherever I want. Wherever might be the loneliest and most peaceful place to rest. But it's never the right place. I never feel lulled. When I wake in the morning, having succumbed at some point, I'm forced to acknowledge that it had nothing to do with the saucer. I guess the fantasy isn't very useful. But it's been years and years. In my mind, it's so well developed. I know every stitch on every pillow in that saucer, is how it feels."

I said, "You can't do that."

He blinked at me. "What?"

"You can't point a fucking gun at people. You can't do that, man!" I was shouting.

And briefly, he collapsed. He inhaled, closed his eyes, bowed his head, and nodded. "I know," he said, still nodding. "I know, I know, I know, I know." For a second he looked just exactly the way he had as a child. Then he pulled me into a tight embrace. "Come here," he said. I stiffened, then relaxed into him. "I'm sorry," he said into my shoulder. "I love you. I'm sorry. I'm really sorry."

I pushed him away, exhaled, rubbed his back. I told him it was all right. I loved him, too. Then I reached to let the seven iron clatter into the golf cart's bed and climbed out.

"Hey," he said, looking up at me, then back at the steering wheel, "good luck this week. Do your best. You never know who might be at these things." He nodded once to punctuate the advice. Then he accelerated, swung the golf cart around in a tight loop so that he faced the opposite direction, ready to drive to the Cottage. "Well, brother," he said. "Good night."

The pedal clinked. He drove up the hill.

Way atop it, a light flicked on in our father's bathroom. In the window, I could just barely make out his hunched silhouette. Ten years, or fifteen, my brother had said. All it takes is imagination.

Later, from my upstairs window, I saw the golf cart's taillights in the fields, by the goat pen. I knew he was there—unlatching the gate with the bag of feed on his shoulder, speaking gently, touching each goat's head in turn.

And hours after that, I felt something nagging under my sleeve. We were midflight, tens of thousands of feet up. I unbuttoned my cuff and rolled it up. It was a tick—head sunk into my flesh, little legs in the air. I held my arm in my hand. When I noticed my seatmate staring down at it, I smiled at her, in apology.

# GHOST IMAGE

Joe Daly—

Come back to me.

I am beaming these thoughts to you. Calling you with them.

With my eyes closed, now, I can see you. As you were when we first met: narrow mustache, bald spot, potbelly. Those dress shirts you wore then—gentle pinks and blues, to match the carpeting and cubicle dividers. Like you'd been born from those corporate halls. And here's your windowless office. Acrid light, swivel chair, coffee-ringed mouse pad. Look, Joe, I can reassemble it all. The Thomas Kinkade wall calendar. Family photo in the Epcot Center frame. Don't these things want to be remembered, now that they're gone? There's your old desktop monitor, with the Dopey bobblehead stuck to its top. That innocent grin—it looks just like yours, Joe.

And now I can see the day, sixteen years later, when you were born. Blood on the floor, blood on the doctor's purple gloves. Holding your mother's leg as she hissed through her teeth. The wet crown of your head coming into the air.

I am beaming these thoughts to you. You're owed more, Joe, but it's a start. I am beaming these thoughts up through the windshield, out of this cockpit. Over the park, across the burning Florida lowlands. Beaming them past the clouds and into the sky. Then back down to you, Joe. My Joe Daly. Wherever you are.

You placed an ad in the campus bulletin: Applicants sought for a short-term, unskilled summer job, formatting two hundred new computers at a large insurance firm in suburban Columbus. Suppose I'd never seen it, Joe? But I did. School was out, my college band needed money to make an EP. I was just twenty-one, an art history major, and sufficiently unskilled. The work was mindless and slow, performed in an unfinished office on the third floor of that purplish spaceship—the kind of business park that was everywhere back then, in the early 2000s: shiny and angular, ringed by blacktop, parked cars in orbit. A futurist concept, I guess. But overly credulous. Devoid of irony. A little nerdy. I myself had never been in an office before, and to me it all seemed so quaint: screened calls, birthday cupcakes, all-team meetings. Golf talk in the late afternoon.

For eleven and a quarter an hour, I was to plug in each new computer tower, open the drive, and insert a CD you had labeled, in blue Sharpie, GHOST IMAGE. The disc lobotomized the computers, making them idiot versions of themselves, recalling nothing. Then it rebuilt them according to your design—the right email client, the right security measures. An army of identical machines. The computers surrounded me in stacks. As they ghosted, I'd stare out the window onto the dumpsters in the loading bay. Robed in the hum of the PCs, hours on end, my mind would lose weight like a helium balloon. I began to wonder what would finally become of a mind, left to its own devices in a place like that.

And when you, Joe, walked in and sat down—in theory to observe my progress, though inevitably to drone on about college hoops, or your new mower, or your uninteresting daughters—I saw that you were far more advanced in that study than I ever hoped to become.

Joe Daly. IT Department Leader. I'd watch as you spoke, convinced that your mind had to be in there, somewhere. There *had* to be a mind or a spirit or ghost inside Joe Daly that was smarter than Joe, more than Joe. Otherwise life was too cruel. Maybe, I thought, our minds are like radios, and consciousness is something we receive on the air. Maybe the rest of Joe Daly—ecstasies, lusts, intrusive thoughts—was lost in static out in the universe.

I wish now, of course, that I could recall every word you said back then—each pleasantry and banal anecdote. I might have missed some clue, something to explain how all this happened. But it's been decades, Joe. That summer feels like another lifetime, and my memories of it like dreams. The only talk of ours that I never did forget was the one about the monorail. It all came back to me again, in fact, just last week—west of Lake Okeechobee, on the floor of that crowded gymnasium, smoke coming in through the vents.

It was August when you told me about the monorail. The stacks had dwindled, ghosted PCs were turning up on desks throughout the building. Hands behind your head, striped in sun from the slatted blinds, you inhaled, stretched, sighed. Then, in a gentle voice, you said: Only two weeks to go until the big back-to-school Disney trip. I nodded, looked away, wished I were elsewhere. It's a special family tradition, you explained. Crowds are light, hotels very reasonable. Two Disney trips a year meant there was always something good on the horizon. You had it all worked out. Still, you *did* sometimes like to imagine that—well, for now, this was just an idea. Something nice to think of. A long shot. *But*—it was only ten years until the girls would be grown and out of the house. And if you could move your money just so—not to mention talk your wife into it—your big dream was to retire early, move down to Disney, and work full-time as a conductor on the monorail. Just ride above the park, all day long. That would be the absolute greatest. You'd do it tomorrow if you could. Because here, at the office, you work your whole life away, and what's it really accomplish? Who are you helping? On the monorail, you'd be part of something good. Taking people to where they truly wanted to be.

The day's last computer finished ghosting. I ejected the disc, put it back in the jewel case.

The conductors wear a uniform, you said. With a real conductor's hat.

It's not big of me, Joe, that I could muster no reply, and now, all these years later, I'm sorry about it. I only watched you with young, pitying eyes, safe in the certainty that I'd never have to run from a life as dull as yours. I would pass through your world clean, like a speeding satellite.

Then I was thirty-seven and about to become a father. That's how I remember it. Your mother, Maureen, was beautiful, though severe, thin lipped, with from certain angles a man's square jaw. Do you believe that the face is a reflection of the mind, Joe? Or maybe that everything is— that the mind is the matrix of all matter, as I think someone once said. I'm watching my own face, mirrored in the windshield of this cockpit. My eyes are heavy and full of blood. My cheeks are sagging, nose pocked, forehead spotted. I've got no choice but to believe it.

I was working at the American Visionary Art Museum in Baltimore when Maureen and I met at one of Dave Orlofsky's four-track parties. The point was to improvise a full-length album, sequentially, with whatever Dave had lying around the apartment. Pots and pans, banjo, Omnichord. By the end of the night the tape had to be full, and no excuses. Dave was then the touring bassist for Nude Amateur; he knew Maureen from the Zen center. I fell hard for her that night—the way she caught the spirit, in that little leather jacket she always wore, doing percussion with a box of pasta, wrapping a dishrag around it to get the tone right. Well, Joe, with your mom—all due respect to her memory—that kind of thing, it was just a big put-on. She got pregnant, packed the leather jacket into a storage bin, and then as if by magic I was whisked out of our city walk-up and into the suburbs, where your grandma Ada helped us buy a pretty green house not far from her own.

You were born in the spring. The dogwoods were in flower. I remember your eyes—how big and clean they were when they'd open. All the dawns you spent at your mother's breast. The way you learned to crawl, your whole body working toward that Mickey Mouse we'd set just past the edge of your blue blanket. Once, maybe nine months old, you woke early from a nap, and I entered the nursery, lifted you from the crib, held you against me in the rocker. You swelled with each breath, slower and richer as you passed back into sleep. A box fan was running; lace curtains held the light. And suddenly I knew that my future self was there with us. I could feel him—a third presence, cohabiting my mind and body, having sailed back on psychic waves, just to relive that perfect, quiet moment.

Are you a father yourself now, Joe? You'll do better with it. I wish I could have relaxed into that life. Tended our garden. But once that early pheromonal fog had worn off, I could see where I was: underneath a suburban kitchen table, picking up avocado slices you'd thrown down there. And I felt that couldn't be right. Because the thing was—I'll tell the truth now, embarrassing as it is—since childhood, I'd had this deep conviction that my life would be one of the special ones. That I was meant for something bigger. It was a feeling; it's hard to explain. But there'd been signs and symbols, synchronicities. And the ability I had with my spine: I could will a bolt of energy up my spine and out through my brain, precipitating a brief psychic bloom—intense awareness of detail in my surroundings, a sense of divine presence. The most beautiful sensation. I can't do it anymore. And just look at me now—raiding abandoned restaurants around the park for canned goods, ducking out of sight of the drones.

But if it's pathetic, Joe, if it's ridiculous, then my pathetic, ridiculous truth is that, even after you were born, and Maureen had gone corporate, and the suburban gallery where I worked ran a show of dog portraits, and I'd grown fat, bitter, and maybe alcoholic, with everything melting into that deathlike American placidity I'd first glimpsed at the office park in Columbus—even then, Joe, when I imagined the future, what I saw was myself, silver maned and open shirted, onstage, in an armchair, fielding softballs about my celebrated life and work. Reception to follow.

I took this eventuality on faith. My aspirations were not particular. Dilettantism was the point. I was an artist in search of a medium. Back then, didn't we all see ourselves that way? Call it the cumulative effect of nineties children's television commercials, or the fact that so many of our teachers were hippies—real, historical hippies. Or the rise of video-gaming, paired with the fall of communism. It could have been something in the water, Joe. I mentioned the college band, Shabby Ruby. Heavy drone music. I played keys—not very well, though it didn't take much technical ability to use the arpeggiator. We'd moved from house shows to clubs, postgraduation, and were talking about getting a van. But then Alan, the guitarist, went to law school, and the third guy wouldn't keep going without Alan. In my late twenties I made ambient sound collages, web comics, rudimentary platformers; in my early thirties I wrote morning pages, took B-complex vitamins to induce lucid dreams, read up on the occult. I paid little attention to my string of jobs, which I viewed as a stopgap. There was my daily life, the straight one, and then my imaginative, ensouled life, developing in parallel, steering me toward the point of embarkation I knew was approaching.

But I waited, and the point of embarkation never came.

You took your first steps out in the yard. By summer's end, you were chasing fireflies. We finally gave up trying to figure out who you looked like. Your flat, serene face and upturned nose—where had they come from? Not me. And even in her baby pictures, Maureen had the hard, under-ripe quality she'd inherited from Ada. We'd decide for a time that you had my father's ears, or Aunt Liz's brows. Then you'd grow, change, and the resemblance would pass. Zooming in on your newborn photos—red and frail, clinging to Maureen in the delivery room—we'd argue over whether it was the same kid down the hall. Sometimes I thought the problem was your name. Wasn't it a poor fit? I asked Maureen if she'd ever known anyone who changed their kid's name.

My sweetest memories run right up against the weird ones. One night, you woke crying. I, tossing and turning myself, went to jostle you back to sleep. You were half in a nightmare. As you wriggled against me in the pitch black, your mouth wet on my neck, I had the distinct impression that I was holding not my son but a wiry, muscular eel.

What happened to those years, between your birth and Maureen's death? Sixteen of the fucking things. The art gallery folded. I found bookkeeping work with a small theater company and spent weekends getting high with my city friends. I said no more kids; Maureen knocked out a wall and redid the kitchen. My hair came in gray, I worried about my erections, the United States defaulted on its debt. But still I read hopefully about late bloomers. Did you know that Philip Glass drove a cab into his forties? When you were thirteen, I converted the attic to my studio and took up painting again. As I worked, I tried to be loose in my body, rolling my shoulders, waving the energy up my spine, like before.

Around that time, I had a dream. It's just past sunset and I'm back in Columbus at the insurance firm. The room is dark, filled with the hum of ghosting computers. Down by the dumpster I see a bonfire built from big sticks, crossed at the top, shooting sparks into the air. And standing beside it is Joe Daly. Wearing a suit of black feathers. Terrified, I sink to the floor, and there I become conscious of a tug between my legs. Hooked directly into my scrotum is an old 32-pin connector cable. It's running to one of the computer towers. Running to *Ghost Image*.

Then you woke me up. You said you'd missed the bus.

The morning was cold and bright, late autumn. By then, the homeless camp on the golf course south of Ardmore was sprawling and unpredictable enough that I liked to take the long way to the middle school. We drove in silence—our particular silence, the one that'd been growing between us for years. I know I wasn't the best dad, Joe. But try to see it my way. First you were loud, messy, and needful; later, a good-natured mediocrity. By that morning you were freckled and overweight, dark puberty fuzz atop your lip. You were a sports watcher. A reader of mass-market biographies on noted tech entrepreneurs. The only music you liked was from video games.

We stopped outside the school. An armed guard in fatigues opened the car door, one hand on his rifle stock.

You bobbed off into that sea of vulgar teens, backpack cinched too high. I sat with that touch of dissociation I often felt, watching your body move, until the guard rapped his knuckles against the trunk.

Safely back home, I walked up the stairs to the attic. That was the year the gallery went under, and I hadn't bothered looking for more work. Maureen was rolling in cash, working under Grandma Ada at Vanguard. And she was in no position, besides, to voice displeasure with me. The young associate with whom she'd been sleeping had driven her to total distraction. The way I remember that year, she was always in the bathroom. I'd bang on the door—could she just pass me my toothbrush, please? And through the sliver from which it emerged I'd catch a glimpse of your mom, flushed and sweaty, phone in hand. Don't be scandalized, Joe. These are the facts of life. He'd break it off for a while, stop responding to her texts, and she'd fall into these depressions. I'm sure you sensed something was wrong. Remember the time she forgot to pick you up from your math tutor, and you had to run home in the rain, and you broke your toe on the buckled sidewalk?

She never lied about the string of young men who followed, and she extended me the same liberties, though I couldn't be bothered to make use of them. I thought her so shameless and needy, with those obnoxious new friends. Suddenly, like a kid, she was taking psychedelics again; she'd come home from the city wearing face paint.

When she died, she was on a high dose of acid. Of course, I never told you that. I wouldn't have known myself if not for Robert, who'd been with her that day in Big Sur. Robert wasn't actually such a bad guy, Joe. He came by the house a few times afterward. We'd sit and drink some beers. The whole thing really shook him up.

Anyway—in the attic, I sat on my stool and looked at my paintings. I'd recently embarked on a major project: remaking individual Thomas Kinkade canvases with the aim of getting something ecstatic into them, softening lines, blurring faces. The fact that I had no technique was exactly the point. To me it was protest art. I'd stay locked in the attic for days. In moments of despair I'd throw the canvases out the big double window, then go to carry them back in, one by one. I knew I wasn't any good, but I came to feel that the real problem was the necessity, in the first place, of something so stubborn as an artistic medium. One day, I hoped, when times were better, a new technology would reproduce and transmit thoughts, sense perceptions, dreams—unmediated interiority itself. Until such time, I'd work on the Kinkades.

But that morning, the morning of my dream, I noticed something. The funny milk-faced fellow I'd begun putting into the paintings, as a running gag—a symbol, in his shallow contentedness, of everything disappointing in life—he was you, Joe. I sat, staring. There you were on one canvas, and another, and another. I hadn't realized I was doing it. Because the face I'd painted was yours, yes—although not as you were. Not as a boy. It was you as you might have looked in middle age. Rounder, balder, mustached.

When your mom died, I went deep, deep, deep into the Kinkades. I was working then through his Disney World series, commissioned in 2006 for the thirty-fifth anniversary of the park. I'd come to feel that putting life into the paintings wasn't daring enough and had moved on to high strangeness and violence—UFOs bombing Cinderella's castle, brother and sis fucking on Main Street, their folks gagging each other with smoked turkey drumsticks. I don't have to tell you it was a bad year. I remember climbing down from the attic, knocking on your door, asking how you were doing. Okay, you'd say, and I'd patter off, noting sometimes with regret that it was three in the morning or some stupid time like that.

Your grandma Ada was around a lot. I'd lie with my ear against the floorboards, her footfalls growing louder until the knock came at the attic door. She was a terribly frank woman, birdlike, with smoker's skin and cold eyes. We'd never really gotten along. But when she suggested that you stay with her for a while, I agreed. It was the right call.

Those next homebound months were a dark time. The thing that still scares me, when I think about Maureen, is this thought I've had—irrational, I know—that maybe the way she experienced it, the way it was for her, she was outside of time. That when it happened she wasn't perceiving time normally, I mean. That maybe for Maureen even now it's like she's drowning.

I told Ada I didn't want to attend Thanksgiving, but she wouldn't let it drop. Ada loved the old rites of secular America—Christmas-card beach photos in matching white, a Halloween costume for the dog, and so forth. Prickly as she was, Ada had a sentimental streak.

I remember that gigantic American flag sticking off her front porch, pointed at me like a lance from behind the perimeter fence where I parked. I stood in front of the camera and buzzed.

It felt weird, walking in, but thankfully, there was little what's-her-name, Liz and Jared's daughter, who took me by the hand, insisting I come see the wobbly paper-ring turkey centerpiece she'd made in kindergarten. My heart swelled. I looked up at Jared—ignorant son of a bitch, I'd always hated that guy—and, yes, she had his nose, his sharp canines, those same raisin-hued recesses under her eyes. She even had that square jaw, the very same that Liz shared with her mother and Maureen.

Then I saw you, Joe. For real, I mean. For the first time.

It's true that you'd shot up that year. To me you looked two inches taller. And the way you still wore it all on your sleeve, poor guy, eyes downcast, talking to Aunt Liz in the next room, gave you an air of sad maturity. But that wasn't all. Your pale blue button-down dress shirt was tucked into slacks. Pleated? What kind of teen, I thought, wears pleats? You'd put on more weight, but oddly, right at your center, so that your belly bulged over your belt. At the very crown of your head—the same one I'd seen pushing out from Maureen all those years ago—an unfortunate premature bald patch grew. And weirdest of all was the little mustache you now sported, clipped tight, with a clean line below your nose.

Joe Daly. There you were.

Ada approached, not so subtly extending a glass of seltzer and lime. And then she made a little speech, which she'd clearly rehearsed. The whole time she looked straight up at my eyes. I could lean on her, she said. She herself was a widow, and we'd both lost Maureen. She said that you needed me, Joe. That I had important work to do with you. The most important and necessary work of my life, of any human life. And though I was lost and bewildered, that work was now incumbent upon me. If I might find some way toward growth in all this, that's where it would be—in you, in what I owed to you. She squeezed my bicep.

But I felt weightless, afloat somewhere between the light fixtures and the ceiling. To realize at once what you've always known—is there a word somewhere for that? What it makes me think of, now, is Dave Orlofsky. Years after we'd lost touch, after I'd stopped seeing my friends, Dave went for a cigarette on his fire escape, fell off it into the alley, and was paralyzed. He lived two different lives—one and then the other. And so did I. But my life had split in two a long time before I knew it. Watching you over Ada's shoulder, I felt astonished and frightened and foolish in some way I didn't understand, couldn't, still don't.

Ada sat me beside you at the table. Little Janie, that was

her name, said grace. Bless our family and our Thanksgiving, and bless my paper turkey and Ms. Murphy for helping make him, bless us all for dinner today, amen. And then Ada led the table through the Pledge of Allegiance. Her insistence on it every year was bizarre. But you know what's funny, Joe? Now I find myself missing it. That was my last old-fashioned Thanksgiving. It was a bad day, and nothing since has been good, but look—we had the pilgrim salt and pepper shakers. We had pie and the gravy boat and turkey-shaped butter.

The meal began. You were talking. They all seemed to want you to talk; they asked you questions. At school, you had joined the Tech Club. You felt at home in the Tech Club. You'd even gotten an extra-credit internship with the IT Department, repairing laptops and tablets. I wanted alcohol, but there was no wine on the table, no one else was drinking, and I grew paranoid, thinking that was all due to me—they were watching me, attempting to manage me. A bad feeling rose up. I couldn't eat, couldn't look at anyone as you spoke, so I stared at Janie's paper turkey, sitting just before me, in profile. Now I could recognize your voice, Joe. Add thirty years, make it deeper, slightly hoarser, and your voice would be his voice. Or his voice was yours—what was the right way to think about it? Sweating, feverish, I excused myself from the table, took my seltzer into the den, poured it out behind the sofa, and filled the glass high with gin from the wet bar. When I returned, I kept my eyes low. It sounded like everyone had stopped eating. A long time passed. Then Jared prompted you to go on about the laptop repairs. You swallowed, sipped from your water glass, and explained that you enjoyed that sort of project-based work. The sense of helping people. And with the long-term economic outlook being what it was, a practical field such as IT seemed like a good bet.

They all knew—they always had. That's what I decided, and it might sound crazy now, but it didn't just then, at that table. They all knew, they'd known your whole life, had conspired somehow to make it so, and Thanksgiving was only a pretext: The day's real purpose was to communicate openly, for the first time, that you were Joe Daly, that they all knew you were Joe Daly, and we had now entered a new phase wherein we would agree to know it, would proceed on the basis of knowing it, though we could never speak it aloud, and my silent presence at the table was my consent.

I got up, went back to the den. Whispers from Jared and Ada, but that was all. Pouring the gin, knocking the spout against the glass, I found that I was drunk. From where I stood, I heard you say that the Tech Club had planned a spring-break trip. You were flying to Orlando. You were going to Disney World. Please forgive me, Joe. I snuck through the kitchen, out the sliding door, and around the side of the house.

It took concentration to drive, but it was doable, totally doable. The roads were violet in the chilly dusk, and after some meandering I found myself in a derelict subdivision beneath buzzing orange streetlamps, relics of the twentieth century, of the sort that I've always associated with my childhood. I put the seat back and conked right out.

In the night, I woke with a monstrous headache and looked through the windshield at the moonless sky. It rippled, like something had been dropped into it, and feeling suddenly upside down I fumbled for the door, certain I'd vomit. But then a light punched through the clouds, brighter and wider until I had to squint, and from within it came two gigantic hands, in a loving, open-palmed gesture of embrace. They hovered an instant, and then the fingers curled back and the hands withdrew into the sky, leaving all as it had been. Peaceful and calm, I fell again into a deep sleep.

In the morning, I drove south. West of Baltimore, I found Route 70 and shot out into the Catoctin Mountains, where I ate a buffet dinner in the little town of Thurmont. Spot-lit steam trays of sugared ham and sweet potatoes, cobbler and rolls, fountain drinks—a second Thanksgiving, my own private one. Then it was west on 68, where the cop cars sat head to toe in the median, and out onto the blue highways. Alfalfa fields, chicken houses, forlorn villages. A billboard near one such place warned that HELL IS REAL. I wondered if it were meant for me, if I had entered hell, and looking back on it I guess that I had—the hell of earthbound ghosts that repeat the same actions, haunt the same spaces.

It was sunset when I found the office park—shuttered,

a chain stretched across the lot entrance. Well, it had been the better part of forty years. Pale weeds grew through cracks in the pavement, far from one another, waiting for death. What a sad thing, I thought, to sprout up that way, only to find yourself choked in hard-set rock. The buildings' glass exteriors had faded from their old royal purple to a pale amber. I shivered. Places have their seasons, too, and here was yours, Joe, in the ruin of winter.

The first three doors I tried were locked. The fourth, around by the courtyard, was propped open with a large stone. Inside it was damp, dark, barren, no furniture apart from some eerily scattered chairs. The carpet was torn up, holes punched through the walls. If I could sit in your office, I thought, I might learn something. Maybe I would stay there for a while. I could meditate, build big fires in the conference rooms, roast the possums and raccoons that nested in the ducts, and with their bones, I'd conduct strange rituals to summon Big Joe, the Joe behind it all, the spirit or essence or force of which you were an avatar, and he would explain everything to me.

But I looked and couldn't find your office. They were all the same.

Exhausted, I sat on the floor and imagined my body as it had felt the last time I'd been in that place. Quick and light. I grabbed my belly, rubbed my chin and cheeks, examined the proof of the intervening years.

Back outside, I wandered around to the loading dock. The place where you'd stood in that terrible dream. Just for fun I picked a third-floor window, imagined that I saw myself peering down from it. Then something in the dumpster caught my eye. With some difficulty I pushed myself up and fell in. It was an Epcot Center picture frame, dimpled and round. Without a photo, blank in its center, it reminded me of a crystal ball. It must have been yours—the same one that had sat to the left of the old desktop monitor, all those years ago. Right? Well, probably not. How many identical picture frames were out there, somewhere, in America? Tens or hundreds of thousands. I thought of all the people whose photos they housed, or once had, all the Epcot frames together.

Where were they?

If you have a car in America, you still have quite a lot. You can get so far-flung so fast that to start over again and again is no sweat. Look for work, find a spot to plug in and take a shower. Those years in my mind are just earth tones blurring by at eighty per, the white stripes rumbling underwheel to the rhythm of *day-lee-JOE, day-lee-JOE.* In hot weather I shared the car with whatever wanted to come in. Once, I opened my eyes before dawn to find a green mantis perched on the tip of my nose. I gasped and flailed, tumbled out the door; it hopped gracefully into the meadow. And once, too, as I reclined in the driver's seat near dusk, a sparrow zipped in one window and out the other, like a shot.

I'd never really seen the Great Plains or the desert

or the Mountain West. There were long, full road days when I'd encounter no other soul, or at least that's how it felt—just driverless convoys, wind farms, automated convenience stores. Unmanned aerial vehicles purring overhead. I spent time in Big Bend, Death Valley, Badlands, Black Canyon. Even then, the people squatting in those places had agriculture, solar arrays. Most were friendly. Once, near Las Cruces, I stopped on the shoulder of a high unmarked ranch road and saw a camp way off, down on the desert floor, a mile out at least; there were horses and wagons and smoking fires, and briefly I didn't know what year it was, what era. My body took the shape of the car. Standing, I'd shrink back toward that seated position, and my arms grew heavy, accustomed to hanging from the wheel. For one full year it rained nonstop, or might as well have. Each time I picked up a truck-stop paper, I'd read about more drivers killed by falling trees. There were bridges out, buckled roads, and when the sky cleared, everything was so green. Green to hurt your eyes.

I didn't have many friends then. But I did make one best friend, and that was Lacey. We both behaved poorly the night we met and that forged a bond between us. She was a little younger, midforties, and wore her black hair chopped short. With her pale complexion and half rings below her eyes, she resembled a raccoon. She even had hands like a raccoon, with little sideways-pointing thumbs. We had a habit of getting into ugly shouting matches, the ends of which I seldom could recall. But in the daylight, when I woke to find her having her morning smoke out on the hood of the car, I'd go sit beside her and we'd pick a new spot on the map.

Lacey was missing her left pinkie finger, and I'd rub that blank place gently when she cried. On the road, she let her long, awful story unfurl. And I told her about you, Joe. I was scared, the first time, but Lacey listened so patiently. This was somewhere south of Tulsa and the night was hot. When I finished, she said she believed me. Then she showed me photos she'd taken of bright little blobs, captured flash-on in the dark, floating over camp-fires or in the corners of rooms, and told me they were spirit orbs. She had lots of theories about spirit orbs. They looked like dust or lens flare to me, Joe, though of course I didn't say so. One early morning in North Dakota the sun startled me awake and I found Lacey in her usual perch on the hood. I rubbed my eyes, spat, and came into the chilly air to sit beside her. Antelope, she whispered. Fifteen or even more maybe. They ran right here in front of the car. She pointed. They darted that way, and one of them jumped right over the other one, fucking leapfrogged him. Her voice was hushed and awed. My eyes welled with tears because I saw she was happy.

We were in a bar, Southern and rural, when Lacey nod-ded toward a guy on a stool in the corner of the room. I looked at him, then back at her, scared and bewildered. She told me later that she knew right away, though she didn't know how. He looked like you, Joe. The guy was staring up at the television, rolling the label he'd peeled from his beer across the tabletop with two fingers. Mustache, bald spot. The same face. But very fat. Drunk. And his eyes were set farther apart than yours. Lacey said that if I didn't go and see, she couldn't respect me. If she knew how to find her sister, she said, she'd move mountains to be with her; she would forgive her everything and go. She was drunk herself. I probably was, too. I watched the guy. From certain angles, I was positive it was you. Then he'd move his head and I doubted. When I stood, I felt dizzy. It seemed like the same music had been playing forever—moody and repetitive, loungy, an alto saxophone mixed low and distorted. I began to cross the room. As I neared, he straightened and sat up a little. Then I was standing over him, looking down, and he looked up at me. It was like you, Joe, but not you. Like you, but changed. In the blue-pink bar light, I couldn't tell his age. His eyes were set wider than yours, yes, but also they were duller. I had always thought you dull, but this was different, true dullness, an absence of light. I asked him if his name was Joe. He hesitated. Then he said that I was close. He was called Joel. His words came out badly formed. Seconds passed. I told him I had made a mistake. I apologized. When I got back to Lacey, I said that I wanted to go; I didn't feel well. But she insisted on one last beer. She was sullen and distant and seemed somehow to blame me for the situation's outcome. She drank the beer, that strange music still playing, and all the while I could feel Joel there behind me, both of us looking at the television, mounted high, muted.

The next time I found a working pay phone, I dialed Ada. My cell no longer worked to reach the northern states, and I hadn't visited in ages, but now and then I still called. Sometimes I'd bail out and hang up when Ada said hello; often, she wouldn't answer. But other times we would speak. Or she would, always in the same weary and remote tone of voice. That pay phone was outside a pancake house. Early evening, a light rain. Lacey smoked in the lot. Ada told me that you had gone north. You were volunteering with a construction unit in Maine, close to Nova Scotia, in a remote place called Limestone, on a defunct Air Force base, where they were building a new city. There had been no change in your feelings. If you became interested in contact, as ever, she would let me know. The rain thrummed on the cars, on the two-lane highway. Lately when I call, there's no ring.

The last time I saw Lacey was in Indiana. We had parked overnight in a field. I woke to find the side door and glove compartment hanging open, papers and maps whizzing over the grass. All the cash we kept rolled up in the sock was gone. But Lacey was a sweet lady who'd lived a hard life and I wish her only happiness.

When the car broke down in Florida, I could tell it was for good. I walked into the grasslands and picked a bouquet of wildflowers to leave under the wiper, put a few things in my backpack, and set off up the road on foot. An hour later, a tan camo Jeep coming the other direction stopped me—flying a green flag, it belonged to one of the militias. A big guy leaned out. He wore an assault rifle strapped to his chest and gave me a hard look from behind wraparound shades. Then he said, I wouldn't head that way if I were you, my man. Wildfires.

That's how I found myself on the floor of that high school gym, drinking watery coffee, wrapped in a foil emergency blanket. There were competing rumors— forced evacuations, or else they were going to pull out and abandon us, no more guardsmen, no more ration kits, only all us hungry people. The Everglades and Big Cypress were burning down south. To the north, fires west of the Wekiva River, all over, scattered, linking together.

I stared helplessly at the map. A part of me had always figured on dying with the car. And maybe I would. Just sit, drink coffee, try to nap, until it happened. But then, tracing my finger along the turnpike, I saw the place I had to go. Getting there might not be easy. But this was destiny. And what I'd learned is that in the dance with destiny, you have to lead.

I found an open seat in a church van headed to Gainesville. A lot of what the driver said made sense to me—if I hadn't been right in the middle of something, I could maybe have imagined riding all the way. They dropped me in Kissimmee and insisted I take an extra boxed lunch.

There was no traffic headed up toward the park, but something romantic in me liked the idea of walking the final stretch, knapsack on my back. It was a long, lonely highway, and it led to an enormous arch, WALT DISNEY WORLD spelled out above it, and below, WHERE DREAMS COME TRUE. But the *i* in DISNEY was missing, and someone had spray-painted over COME TRUE in a big, mean hand so that it read WHERE DREAMS FUCK YOU. The palms stood perfectly still in the weird, hazy air. From then on, when I heard a car coming I'd duck out of sight.

The ticket booths were abandoned, gates locked, but a nearby fence had a big hole in it. I came up on the park through a ring of shrubs and garbage. It was sad, Joe, to see what had happened. Everything was in shadow. There were people here and there but they looked either confused or menacing, traveling in packs. The buildings and rides were cracked and weathered. A spray-painted swastika crossed the shuttered doors of a souvenir shop. I thought of my old Kinkade paintings, and for one panicked instant, I wondered if I were responsible, somehow, for all of this—myself, or others like me. Up ahead loomed that iconic pockmarked globe, the one I knew from your picture frame. It drew me in, step by step, until I was right under its grand banner: SPACESHIP EARTH. I entered, felt my way along a dim corridor, its walls depicting in mural the evolution and achievements of man. But it grew darker, and I found the interior unattended, the little cars silent and empty. From the bowels of the place I thought I heard laughter, and the sound, together with a gust of cold air from deep in the tunnel, pricked the hairs on my neck.

Back in the light of day I looked for the monorail. Soon I found the track up ahead of me, hanging in the air. And at length a train did come clanking along. Its movements were labored and rough, but then all at once it would lurch and, for an instant, sail with real elegance. It's not that I expected you, Joe, to be sitting up front when the mono-rail creaked into the station. But still, I was heartbroken to see that there was no conductor at all—only a computer panel behind dark glass. The cockpit door was stuck half open. I wedged myself through as the thing jerked forth. "It's a Small World" piped from a speaker above me, the melody subject to grotesque de-tunings as the monorail stalled and started, again and again. The fires glowed on the horizon.

I looped the park for hours, focusing my psychic ener-gies on finding you. I let my brain go light, tried to roll the energy up my spine like before; I felt that here in this place I might get to some version of you even without you, to Big Joe Daly, a Joe Daly of the mind.

And as the sun set, the reflection of the cockpit's inte-rior grew stronger in the windshield than the view of the park, and I began to make you out, little by little, seated there beside me.

Joe, I said, and my old eyes filled with tears.

You were ghostly in the glass. I strained to see if you were Joe as we'd first met, Joe as my child, Joe in the pres-ent or the past. But you were more than that—all possible Joes, in your uniform and proud conductor's cap, radiat-ing peace, a brilliance waving from your eyes to my heart.

If I blinked, I worried, you might be gone, so I stared until the color drained and the lines bent. You were serene. I stammered, stopped, began again. I said, Joe, this will sound funny, maybe, but—somewhere in Louisiana a while back I saw a graveyard. There was a marker for a boy who'd died in the eighteen hundreds. His parents had inscribed it—let's see—*An innocent soul trod the earth blithely . . .* no. *His soul trod blithely the fair earth*—no, I don't know. But it had *trod blithely*, Joe, and it put me in mind of you. Because isn't that you, to a tee? My blithe treader.

In the reflection, I thought I saw you smile.

I told you how I stood there among the stones and tried to throw a rope out to you with my mind. And the rope went different directions. I said I didn't know what it meant, Joe, that your life sprang from mine. But that I was tired, now, from thinking it over. When I was young, I said, I didn't know how long life takes, or what it does to you as you live it. But now I do know. And that's what you need to understand, Joe. I am your supplicant. I'm on my hands and knees. I'm yours. Your buddy, your father, your disciple. All of it. Please. Please, Joe.

My eyes were shut tight and brimming.

I opened them. In the glass, you were fading away. There were stars out.

After you'd gone, I studied my face in the windshield. It's ugly now. But Joe, it's all I've got.

A pack of deer ran beneath the monorail one early morning. We stayed together until the track curved off. I watched them trot up into Spaceship Earth and never saw them come out, so I know they're safe and cool still. Sometimes I wonder—if the world's remaining Joes came there, too, in search of sanctuary, would I know mine from the crowd? And would you know me? When you were young, we would tell you, Samuel, if you get lost, don't move. Just stay where you are until you're found. I'm sorry to use that name, Joe. I know it isn't yours. But isn't it funny, how right it nearly was? It means "name of God." Someday the fires will be gone, the lowlands burned clean, everything fallen away. I'll wait here. Come find me.

# NEIGHBORS

Not long after our twins turned three, my wife, Anna, accepted a transfer to the West Coast. The opportunity was lucrative, but that wasn't why we were eager to go. Anna had spent that March and April involved with another man, a colleague, someone whose name I'd never heard before she told me. She said it was a terrible mistake, that it had only made her hate herself, and that this person had now begun almost to frighten her, continuing to call after she'd told him to stop, declaring that he'd leave his family, insisting on speaking with me. I felt sorry for her. The episode was the culmination of a long withdrawal we'd each made from the other—for some time, our mutual unhappiness had felt like too delicate or intimate a subject to broach. I knew I wasn't blameless. And our kids were so young. The hard-to-fathom part, really, was just that she'd hidden it from me. It felt so old-fashioned, predicated on such a rigid understanding of who we could be together. In bed, in the dark, I told her that if we wanted to try again, we would have to redraw the map. We spent the days that followed talking more openly than we had in years—about our girls, our childhoods, old lovers, doubts and desires we'd each thought too fragile to admit.

In San Francisco, we found a house in the Outer Sunset, four blocks east of the Pacific. The neighborhood was row after row of small townhouses, all the same footprint, in sun-bleached pastels. Most of them had been built in the thirties, and not long before that, the place had still been called the Outside Lands—desolate and windswept, just scattered people growing vegetables in the shifting dunes. We'd been warned against the Sunset due to the cold and fog that often settled there. But on clear days, we woke to pristine ocean views. There was a walking path down by the beach that led north to Golden Gate Park and south to the zoo. The girls would run ahead, holding hands, leaning close sometimes to whisper, and we'd push the stroller behind them. They could talk with just the barest application of language; they really did have that preternatural closeness I'd always heard about in twins but had never had the opportunity to observe. After they'd gone to bed, Anna and I would sit on the deck with some wine or a joint and watch the sunset. It felt good to be there. I told her which of my friends I'd always been in love with. She told me that she'd never stopped silently reciting the nightly prayers she'd learned as a child. I asked her once what she'd wanted from her relationship with this other person, what she'd hoped might be possible. The question made her laugh. She said, Ecstasy, a miracle—I don't know.

Weekdays, Anna dropped the girls at school before driving into town. I made an office in our downstairs mother-in-law unit, built into the garage's back corner, and stayed home. Soon I felt attuned to the place, the way it sounded and felt across time. Surfers jogged down the hill every morning, carrying their boards. Deep in the night, sometimes, the sinking moon lit up the ocean. People were friendly. Hal and Eleni were our neighbors to the right. Early on, they rang our bell with flowers and a cheerfully annotated map of the neighborhood, printed from Google in black and white. Across the street was another young family who seemed very nice; we resolved to all take our kids to the playground someday but never did. And in the house to our left, there was an elderly woman who lived alone. Hal said her name was Bing.

Weeks passed before we met Bing, though we often heard her—she had a booming cough and a landline phone with an old-fashioned clapper that seemed to be mounted on our shared wall. All night long, she played her television at earsplitting levels. I imagined she slept in front of it. Sometimes I'd see her from our bedroom window, hanging laundry on her back patio. She was hunched and overweight and used a walker, and the whole sad spectacle—the way she'd labor to get the basket of wet clothes out the door at the back of her garage, let it drop onto the plastic table there, hang each article, one by one—was hard to watch. I've always been a bad sleeper, and sometimes, lying awake at four or five, a sudden glare through the window would startle me: the motion-activated spotlight over Bing's back door. I imagined that if I got out of bed and walked to the window I would see her, on the patio, dressed for the day, making her slow, lonely progress at something or other.

One Saturday in September, on our way out the door to Point Reyes with the girls, we found a conversion van parked in front of Bing's house. A man our age, forty or so, was there, helping Bing up into the van. It was our first opportunity to say hello, so we loitered in our driveway as he braced his shoulder against her, rubbing her back very tenderly as she climbed, her entire body trembling. Trying not to watch, I set my eyes on the walker, which stood alone on the sidewalk. The man got Bing seated, helped buckle her, then jogged over to introduce himself. All through our conversation, Bing smiled out at us, leaning forward to see through the van's side doors. His name was Henry, he was Bing's youngest son, he'd grown up there in the house beside ours and now lived in Stateline, Nevada, where he was a rock climber. I thought he looked too put together for that, with his striped golf shirt tucked into khaki shorts, but the van, I saw, was rugged and full of gear. In that Californian way to which I was still becoming accustomed, Henry seemed authentically pleased to meet us. He wanted to know if I played tennis. There were courts behind the high school, he had his racket in the van, he'd only come home to take Bing to the doctor, but he'd be around all weekend. Henry was well-built, in easy possession of his body; he carefully and politely divided his attention between Anna and me as he spoke. I thanked him, with regrets. I'm pretty sedentary, I said, excepting walks in the woods, things like that. Sure, he said, no problem. When Anna called out to Bing to say that she'd raised a very nice son, Bing responded warmly in Chinese from the back of the van. Before we left, Henry asked if we might exchange numbers. His father had died a year earlier, his brother lived in Denver and his sister in New York, and his mother was stubborn about her independence. It would be a comfort to know there was someone just next door.

Then one morning in March, I was at my desk when a sound that had nagged me as I read from my laptop drifted to the center of my attention: Bing's phone. It had been ringing incessantly, I realized, half a dozen times or more. It stopped, a minute passed, then it started again. I stood, stretched, walked out of my office, into the garage, and through the door to the foyer, where I pressed my ear to the wall. When the phone rang again, I could feel it in my face. And there too was the sound of Bing's television, played at its soaring overnight volume. But now it was close to noon.

I climbed the stairs, opened the door to our bedroom, and walked to the window. No laundry on Bing's line. It was misty and cold, a dark shelf of clouds seated atop the ocean. I felt tired, as I always did that time of day; I was fully remote, working East Coast hours. And I knew that, when I checked my phone—which, to keep from distraction, I always left upstairs, plugged into the kitchen wall—I would find messages from Henry. It was inevitable. He'd explain that he couldn't get in touch with his mother and was growing worried. His request that I knock on her door would be apologetic but insistent. And when she didn't answer—of course she wouldn't; why should she answer her door but not the phone?—he'd tell me where to find a key. Soon I would be on the other side of the wall, slowly climbing Bing's stairs, calling her name. I had a bitter feeling about it, like this outcome, this moment, had been certain since I'd first seen Bing, and by extension long before that—since we'd found our house in the Outer Sunset, or since Anna had received the offer to go to California. I watched the ocean a moment longer, then walked into the kitchen for my phone.

Bing's house was a bone-yellow. There were no succulents in the ground out front, no gourds or pots or small cheerful things. All the shades were drawn. I thought she had put her garbage bins out on Tuesday, though I couldn't be certain. A few months earlier, I'd seen Bing from our kitchen window, shuffling back from the curb with no walker and the recycling still up by her garage. I'd gone down to offer my arm. She took it, smiling, and we walked together. When I commented on the day, which was cold but clear, she nodded, said something I couldn't understand, then put her eyes back on the ground. I looked into the open garage. There was a car inside, an ancient black Mercedes that had clearly been many years off the road. There were cardboard boxes wilted with moisture, newspapers in short stacks, unused gardening tools on the wall.

Now I rang the bell, then pounded on the iron gate—most of the houses had them, small gated entryways. No answer, I texted Henry. And as my screen registered his typing, I jogged over to Hal and Eleni's and rang their bell. No one home. The driveway across the street was empty.

My phone buzzed. *I can't reach anyone else nearby. There's a key under the flat stone beside the walk. Again am so sorry but would you please?* Now whatever thoughts of protest I had—that this wasn't my business, that Henry was the one who'd left his poor invalid mother to scale cliffs in Tahoe, and that someone else should be appointed for this, not me—ran on a distant parallel track in my mind. The key was there, pressed by the stone into the pale dusty soil. I had to wrestle it some in the lock, but then the gate sprang open and fell inward.

Battered sneakers sat in pairs by the entryway's wall, old junk mail lay on the ground. I knocked on the wooden inner door. I called out, Bing? This is Tom, your neighbor.

No answer. But the inner door was unlocked.

The sound of the television, caustic at that volume, broke over me as I entered. The lights were off, the air close. It was clear that the house's layout was identical to ours: a foyer off the garage on the ground level, living space up on the second floor. I put my hand on the banister at the bottom of the stairs. I'm coming up, I yelled, though I knew how absurd it was to do so. I would climb the stairs, surface into the living room, and find Bing dead on the sofa in the television's changing light.

My lips and face were numb, I had a sense of moving farther out of myself with each step, and when I did find Bing, it was almost exactly as I'd imagined—though it was an armchair and not a sofa, and she was seated upright. But what I saw first, before any of that, was the man by the window on the far side of the room. The curtains were drawn, lights off, and because I couldn't make out his features, I'd thought he was deep in shadow. Then a commercial for tile cleaner threw vivid blues and whites across the room, and I saw that he was wearing something over his head—a tight-fitting black sleeve that covered him entirely from the neck up, something like Lycra, without eye or mouth holes. Apart from that, he wore a gray hooded sweatshirt, zipped up, and dark jeans. He stood very still, hands at his sides, facing Bing.

There was no question that Bing was dead. You'd never mistake it. Her eyes were half open, lips parted, hands in her lap and upturned. She wore a thin white robe, feet on the ottoman, and the robe fell open above her knees. I looked quickly. The skin on her thigh shone like pearl.

I can remember a confused impulse to smile and apologize to the man for intruding. There were what looked like paint flecks on his jeans, and my mind supplied the rationalization that he could be a handyman. But of course that wasn't right. More likely he was a burglar. Hal had warned me about the roving professionals who loved these old houses; they could drill through the garage doors, trip the wires that ran to the electric openers, steal bikes, tools, anything, and be gone in seconds. And yet nothing in the house appeared to have been disturbed. The man held nothing in his hands. He hadn't run, or made any moves, threatened me in any way. The front gate had been locked and the spare key in its right place. I'd seen no hole drilled through the garage door. Unless he'd snuck in through the back—difficult to do, all the yards were fenced off, there were no alleyways—I had no idea how he'd entered the house.

My phone buzzed in my hand. Henry calling.

What I wanted was to turn and run down the stairs and out into the street. I would go until my chest burst. But I felt paralyzed by the man, by the extraordinary volume of the television, and by Bing. And what if he were violent, this person? I guessed I couldn't turn my back on him. Still, I understood that some action was incumbent upon me. We couldn't stand there forever. So despite it all, I raised my voice over the television and said, I'm Tom. Henry asked me to come.

The commercial changed again. The room grew dark, then light.

I nodded toward Bing. I said, Henry asked me to check on her.

Across the room, the man shifted on his feet.

Bing seemed newly dead. There was no odor, nothing like that. It wasn't some awful spectacle, just a fact needing attention. And faced with this man's presence, I found myself thinking very clinically. I'd told him I was going to check her, and so now I had to—check for breath, or a pulse, even if there was no point in doing so. I'd never really taken anyone's pulse. I had the idea of taking my own, to rehearse, but I found that I didn't want him to see me do it. My tongue and throat were dry, the numbness spreading over my head.

I told him I was coming now.

As I moved into the room, he took several steps sideways and back, and in that way we maintained roughly the same length of floor between us. Just as in our house, the kitchen and living room were contiguous, split by a wall with open doorways at either end, west and east. He was hovering now at the eastern threshold, where the floor changed from carpeting to linoleum.

I'd only ever stood beside a dead body at a funeral, and I'd never touched one. But I touched Bing's neck with two fingers, like I'd seen it done in movies. Her skin was cool and not unpleasant, and my eyes moved to a framed photo on the wall—Bing and family in younger days. Henry was easy to pick out, though Bing herself was nearly unrecognizable: slimmer, radiant, standing straight unaided. The pleasant-looking man beside her, smiling without showing his teeth, must have been her husband. They all stood around a restaurant table, in suits and dresses, hands on the chairbacks.

To the man, I said that she was dead.

I flushed when I said it, looking into his shoulder to avoid the sight of his face. Even in the low light the fabric must have been sheer enough to see through. He seemed to be tracking my movements—like an owl, or an insect.

I told him I would now have to call the authorities. Before I do it, I said, I'm going to turn off the television. Then I will open the curtains to let the light in.

The remote control sat on Bing's armrest. Once I'd pressed the power button, I saw I'd chosen the wrong order of operations: I would have to cross the floor in near-total darkness. I felt dizzy, doing it; I imagined him striking from the left. But I kept my composure, and when I'd pulled back the curtains, drawn the blinds, and let the day's meager light in, he was there, as before. He'd moved back again, a few steps, through the doorway and into the kitchen. We were now a little closer to each other. And I could see—that the armchair was a maroon suede, and that the couch beside it was covered in plastic. The tray to Bing's right held the last of a meal.

I held the phone high and watched him as I dialed.

And he began taking long, slow steps backward, deeper into the kitchen. The woman who came onto the line asked what was my emergency. I began to explain, but he passed from sight—behind the dividing wall, relative to my position. The operator asked if Bing was breathing. I couldn't answer; I was too startled by his sudden absence, which was even worse than having him there before me. In five quick steps, I entered the kitchen on a sharp line from the window. There he was, still moving backward, passing Bing's refrigerator. The operator told me to begin chest compressions. Now I matched each step the man took with one of my own. I couldn't let him out of my sight again. I told the operator that Bing was stiff and cold and that I didn't want to break her ribs—all of which was true. He was nearing the kitchen's western end. No, I replied to the operator, I had not been present at the time of death. Yes, I was able to remain at the scene. He moved backward through the doorway and into the living room, by the top of the staircase, where I had entered. Here was his chance to descend the stairs and exit the house—that's what he'd been doing, I reasoned, trying to leave without crossing my path.

But he didn't do it. He kept on through the living room, still taking those long, backward steps. He was making a circle. The operator asked if I had any indication that the death was not natural. I didn't know what he was an indication of. It's not that I thought he'd killed Bing, or that anyone had. But he was no handyman. Nor could I believe any longer that he might be a burglar. I hated and tried to avoid seeing the place where his nose pressed against the fabric, and the weird hollow at his mouth.

The death appears to have been natural, I said into the phone.

Then the operator asked if I were alone in the house. I was moving now past Bing, and he was by the window again, his hands pale white in the light there.

I said yes.

It's just you and the deceased, the operator asked, to confirm.

He passed again into the kitchen. I followed.

I said yes again—out of concern for myself, certainly, though I also felt a protective responsibility toward Bing, and toward the house. I wanted no confrontation with him; I just had to get through this.

Other voices were now on the line, impassive, distorted by static—a dispatcher, coordinating with police and EMTs. Help was on the way. The operator asked me to wait on the line with her. I didn't see that as an option, so I ended the call. To the man, I said, Okay—they're coming now. And once I'd heard myself say it, I realized it was true. The words buoyed me. All this would be over soon. They're coming, I repeated. He passed the refrigerator again. I would steer him back toward the stairs. He had to go. This time, I thought, he would of course go down.

And when he didn't, I saw how very small was my understanding of or purchase over all this. I began to panic. He moved past the television, toward the window. Our circuit was unbroken. The repetition had the character of a nightmare. I told him he'd be arrested, but it came out in a pleading tone, and anyway, I wasn't sure I believed it. The police, walking up those stairs and into this—it was like two incompatible realities. And it might still be eight or ten or twenty minutes before they arrived. He knew that time belonged to him. I wanted to sink to the floor and put my head between my knees, but I had the terrible thought that he would just keep on in his bizarre movements, passing me each time he repeated the circle.

Bing's landline rang. The sound scared me badly. We'd been right, it was mounted on our shared wall, in her kitchen, directly across from where he now stood. As the phone kept ringing, it struck me that he'd been there with that sound all morning—and just as heedless of it, probably, as he appeared now. Something about that terrified me. How long *had* he been in the house? I felt I couldn't rule out days, or weeks. When he neared the stairs again, it occurred to me that I might push him. Two hands hard in the chest, or one in the chest and the other at his throat, and he'd fall. Maybe he'd break his neck. The numb feeling covered my entire body and seemed to spread into space around me. Here was the open top of the staircase. I gathered my breath, tensed my shoulders. But I couldn't do it. Next time, I told myself. I had one whole repetition of the loop to get my nerve up.

He moved past Bing, past the television. I felt as if pulled along blindly behind him. There was a bookshelf by the window. Approaching, I scanned it for implements. A heavy brass bookend looked like the best thing, and once I'd reached the shelf, chest heaving and vision clouding, I picked it up.

But then, down through the window, I saw the ambulance. Pulling up to the curb.

Two EMTs got out. I knocked on the glass.

There was the sound of the door from below and then feet on the stairs. I stayed still, and he sank deeper into the kitchen until he was gone from view. I watched the far doorway, the western one, to see if he'd emerge. But he didn't.

The EMTs were a man and a woman, dressed in blue, the

man with a clean-shaved head and tattoos down his neck, the woman with close-cropped hair. They went straight to Bing, searching for any ghost of breath or heartbeat. They paid no attention to me. I couldn't conceive of what I might say to them—that someone else was here, yes, but how to render an explanation beyond that? I thought it over, watching the wall that separated me from him.

The kitchen was all done in yellow. Yellow-print linoleum flooring, pale yellow counters. There were apples in a mesh basket hung from the ceiling, a cereal box beside the toaster. The dishwasher was ajar. And there was an open door in the wall, one that before had been closed. I would have taken it for a narrow pantry, but now I could see it was a back staircase, cramped and twisting, leading down to what I knew was the garage. The staircase looked illegal, not to code; the wood was unfinished and I had to turn sideways to enter. I felt for a switch, found none, and began to descend, not entirely certain that the steps would hold my weight. The door fell shut above me. In the dark, my breathing grew louder. The brass bookend was wet in my hand. Now I could see nothing, and the texture of the air changed, it was damp and cool and had a taste. Finally, reaching with my foot for the next step, I stumbled. I'd come out at the bottom, into the garage.

It was pitch-black. I moved in tiny shuffling steps, hands out in front, and inhaled sharply when they landed on something. The Mercedes, covered in dust and cobwebs. I braced against it, holding the bookend tight, breathing hard. I could feel him there with me, like the dark was a substance that joined us. I thought, This is it, now he's going to do it, though I didn't know what it was. I kept expecting my eyes to adjust, for the car's outline to emerge. But the darkness was total. Total darkness is very rare. I set the bookend down on the hood. Then I took my hands away from the car. I let them rest at my sides. The garage became vast. Anna had said once that it fascinated her to have the ocean so near—it was like infinity just outside our bedroom windows. I felt something similar in the garage, the perceptual illusion of boundlessness. I no longer needed to announce or explain myself. There was nothing to study or question. And I was too scared to think. In fact, it sometimes seems that I've only applied conscious thought to that moment retroactively. I took a breath and held it. This paradoxical calmness came over me. And what I felt, then, was that my life was not in me but diffused across the darkness, which was an unbroken field containing everything. Me and him. Bing. Anna, the girls. Everything. And so no matter what happened next, there could be no consequence, because I had no identity separate from that field. No one did, nothing did. Everything just was, together, without boundaries or names. This appeared to me as a plain description of reality and not a moral or personal judgment. I had never felt anything like it, and nor have I since.

A door opened, and light flooded the garage. A police officer stood there in the foyer. Blinking, looking around, I saw I was alone. What I assume, though I'll never know, is that the man went out the back door and was gone before I'd even started down the stairs.

That afternoon I sat at my desk, looking over the back-yard and down the hill to the ocean, until it was time to walk up the hill and collect the girls. Henry knocked on our door early that evening. He had driven from Tahoe. I was prepared to face accusations, I almost confessed the whole thing to him in the doorway before he'd said a word, but instead he wrapped me in a bear hug, chin pressed into my shoulder. That night I couldn't sleep. Around four, Bing's motion light flashed on and lit our room. Hal and Eleni brought over two loaves of banana bread in the morning. Anna stayed home from work. We dropped the twins at school and then walked up the coast. There were crows everywhere, more than usual. That was a strange thing about the neighborhood, the number of crows. They were enormous and severe against the pastel houses and beach and sky.

The day was bright but windy, the path uncrowded. I told Anna how I'd touched Bing's neck, and about the EMTs and police, and the morticians who had come last to wheel out the body. I told her about the photo of Bing and her family on the wall. And then I told Anna that there had been someone else in the house when I arrived. Up until that instant I hadn't quite known whether to say it, and when I heard the words leave me, I felt nervous, almost ashamed, in a way I couldn't quite make sense of. It was just that what had happened seemed untranslatable—to the bright Pacific morning, the sound of the surf, to Anna or anyone else.

She asked what I meant. Who was it? I said I wasn't totally sure. Where in the house? Upstairs, in the living room, by the window. What was he doing? What did I mean, by the window? I felt my neck and ears flush, and one of those mild dissociative clouds passed over me—how strange, I thought, to be there in California, far from what I'd known. I didn't understand what had happened at Bing's, or how to talk about it, and I still don't, which is why I think of it often. The problem, now, is that I can remember that moment in the garage, but not the feeling of it. It's grown too distant. On occasion, I've come close—when falling asleep, or on the highway, by myself, and once in an elevator.

A bicycle was coming quickly up from behind us. Look out, I said, and stepped to one side of the path. Anna moved to the other. We waited for it to pass. I felt tired and sullen looking at the ocean, like my life had gone on too long. I wished I were alone; I thought how simple things might have been if only she'd never told me.

When we started walking again I said, I think he was a handyman. He must have been there to work. I guess he'd had a key. But there'd been a language barrier. That was all. I'd only wanted to mention it. She asked if he'd spoken with the police. No, I said, he'd left before they arrived. She asked what Henry had said about it. I shrugged and told her it hadn't come up. Anna frowned and said she didn't understand—what I was saying sounded really weird. There's nothing *to* understand, I told her. It wasn't important. And, if she didn't mind, I felt ready to change the topic.

I asked her whether she was hungry. We went and had a meal at a nice café on Judah Street.

That summer was cold and dreary for weeks on end. Henry didn't plan on selling the house, so it just sat there, vacant. I found it harder and harder to focus at my desk, just on the other side of that wall. By August, we'd made up our minds not to stay in San Francisco. There were lots of reasons for it. Anna and the girls went first, on a red-eye. I spent another week selling some furniture, tying up loose ends. I still had Bing's spare key. The night before I left, I walked next door to her house with the intention of entering. It was ten or eleven, the sky steely overhead, clouds low and unbroken. The neighborhood was silent. I stood looking through the gate, holding the key, trying to get the nerve up. It was just an ordinary house, I told myself, an ordinary garage. I put the key into the lock, turned it, pushed the gate open. Then a car started down our block. I thought I'd wait for it to pass, but instead the car slowed, then pulled into the driveway beside ours. It was Hal and Eleni. I stood with one foot inside Bing's open gate, not at all sure how to explain myself. But Hal just got out of the car and waved. Eleni opened the garage and started rolling out the bins. I closed the gate, locked it, and walked to meet them. We all spoke pleasantly for a while.

## THE NEW TOE

I was on the lidded toilet, head in hand, when my two-year-old spun around in the tub, leaned back, raised his legs from the water, and planted both feet on the tiled wall to reveal, there on his left foot, a new toe. There was no mistaking it. You wouldn't have had to count.

Buddy, I said, your foot—but he spun again, sat up, filled the blue whale pitcher with water, and poured it onto the bathmat. I said, No—water stays in the tub. *Why?* he asked, and I said, Because it makes a mess, that's why, you know why.

Now he sat with the left foot tucked under him. I rolled up my sleeve and said, Pal, come here a sec. He squirmed away, shouting, *You can't!* I grabbed hold of the foot and pulled it from the tepid water. There it was. The new toe, as slippery and delicate as the others, sat crowded between the pinkie and what should have been—what had been?—the fourth.

You must pay attention to moments like that. Something, all at once, where before there was nothing. I had the sense of being in two different places: on the toilet at bath time, yes, but also at a point of departure. We were entering a zone of genuine possibility.

I squeezed the baby wash into my hand.

A new toe like that—what could explain it? It was important to come to some understanding there. Because I would have to tell people—the pediatrician, his day care—and in doing so, I'd be made to account for the toe. I would be answerable to it, as I was answerable to every aspect of his life, as a steward of his growth and good health and general success as an organism. And the toe had only just appeared, out of the blue; I knew next to nothing about it. As a birth defect, of course, it might have been perfectly ordinary. But I didn't have the luxury of such a clear-cut explanation. I thought back to the moment, before the bath, when I'd peeled his orange socks off. If the toe had been there, I certainly would have noticed. True, I was exhausted—he'd been up multiple times every night that week—and maybe I wasn't the best or most reliable observer. But I felt sure there'd been no new toe before the tub. And if that were right, then the toe was less than fifteen minutes old. It must have just sprouted.

But then, I thought, rubbing down his chest and struggling arms, that couldn't be. Because who had ever heard of such a thing? No one. By any conventional measure, it was impossible, and even putting that aside, there were logical issues here. For example, you'd think he'd have felt it shooting up and out of his little foot. I tried to imagine the sensation—painful, or itchy, or startling, anyway. Like teething perhaps. And yet there he was, in the water, playing now with his pirate ship, without a care in the world. Besides, if he'd really sprouted a new toe, then why should that be the end of it? The rules had changed, in that case. We were now in a sprouted-toe world, and the door was open to all kinds of wacky shit: toes all over his body, sudden extra toes on, say, ten other children from around the world, and together they would have to, I don't know, do something extraordinary one day. I looked up at the closed bathroom door. A white towel hung there on a hook. It might be weirder. The toe might be the least of our concerns. Beyond that door might be a set of conditions so startling that, the instant we stepped out, we'd forget all about the toe. We could be floating in space, for all I knew, just a bathroom in a void.

I leaned over on the toilet, opened the door, peered out. No void.

Well, I decided, I was wrong, then. I had to be. Because the toe was conceptually unassimilable. And that meant that the problem wasn't with his foot. The problem was with me. I was mistaken. Overtired, depressed, bored. I pressed the heels of my hands into my eyes until I saw colors. He opened and closed the drain repeatedly. The new toe was not possible. Therefore, the new toe did not exist. I blinked, stared at it. I touched it again. I thought, Okay, look, if the toe were both there and not there, then it would be, it would have to be, subject to a different kind of approach. It might be *real* but not physically real—*there* but not literally there. Aloud, to no one, I muttered, Hear me out. Imagine a third path, between here and not-here. You might start down that third path like this: Why a toe? Like, of all things, why that? What's connoted by a toe? Yes, this seemed exciting, this seemed fruitful, and I thought, Well, toes are agents of balance, offering supple points of connection to the ground. Toes are flexible. They grasp. Toes operate as a collective; they—

*Crash you!* he shouted, slamming his pirate ship down onto the water. My pants got all wet. And, toweling myself off, I thought, No, that's not fruitful; it's idiotic. It was a toe, a real toe, now breaching the yellow water, beside the rubber octopus. It was no figment. We were right back to sprouted. And why did that feel so awful? Because, somehow or other, I guessed I'd fucked up. I *would* have to call the pediatrician, and the day care, and others, many others. They'd want to know about the moment I'd noticed it. There would be questions about the delay that was, even now, growing between that moment and the first instance, whatever it was to be, of assertive parental action on my part. Hang on, they'd all say. You thought it might be "fruitful" to try a "nonliteral" approach?

I scooped him up. I pressed him to me, pulled the towel from the door, kissed his wet head. He was such a beautiful boy. I loved him to death. I carried him out, dropped him giggling onto the bed, smiled down at him. The poor little thing.

Trains or dinos, I asked, meaning pj's, and he said, *Trains!* I reached down and took hold of the foot, bent close, peered at the toe, looked up at his face. Then I took the toe between my thumb and forefinger. This little piggy, I said, and twisted it hard to the right. He shrieked and rolled away, looked up at me with real hurt in his eyes. Kiss it, make it better? I asked, and he nodded. I bent my lips to the extra toe. This was all so horrible. I hated myself, hated being myself.

In the cupboard above the sink was the baby Benadryl. I drew a dose into the plastic syringe. Then I opened the Tupperware with all the weed stuff and dug around for the gummies. Last, under the sink, the rubber bands and wire cutters.

Special dessert, I said, and he snatched the gummy and ate it up. Now sleepy juice.

Like a little bird, he opened his mouth for the syringe.

And tonight, I told him, you get to read as many books as you want.

Ma and Pa Pickles are going on a picnic. Here comes Ma with the picnic basket. Please hurry up, Ma! He lay on my chest, moving his whole head to take in the pictures. In their convertible, the happy pigs drove through town and onto the highway, past a worksite—*Excavator,* he said, pointing—and up the icy mountain, where the water-melon truck lost its load, and then down to the beach, and the Pickles family ate and bathed and sunned together. I felt jealous of them, the Pickleses, in their sprawling, well-manicured scenario.

By the time I closed the book, he was heavy and still.

Buddy? I said, and let him roll onto the bed—as white as milk, the right eye closed more than the left. He'll be fine, I said aloud, and kept saying it, bunching the towel under his left ankle, rolling the train pajamas to the knee, cinching the thickest rubber bands around the foot's middle.

Buddy, I said. Hey, buddy. I took up the wire cutters. Hey. Buddy.

Just a trace of blood and a bit of hollow bone, like a quill.

See, I said. It was hardly anything in the first place. No problem.

But I wasn't feeling so hot. I rolled the toe in tissues and flushed it down the toilet. And then I bundled his left foot in five socks: two Batman, two bananas, one Elmo. I picked him up, stood swaying with him in my arms, saying, You're okay, you're okay, and then I turned out the lights and lowered him into the crib. Felt glad it was too dark to see. Reached out again, the crib was gone.

Then the floor went. Now do me, please, I said, falling already, and as I fell, I thought, Oh, my fucking God, yes, yes, here it comes—

# MOUSETRAPS

At the end of an aisle of bolts and nails, I turned the corner and came upon the boy. No older than fifteen, I guessed, in black slacks and a gray Rugolo's Hardware golf shirt. He stood all caved in, shifting his weight back and forth, hair pressed to his scalp with some ointment that shone under the fluorescent tubes.

I cleared my throat. "I'm looking for mousetraps. The kind that don't kill?"

He frowned, cocked his head, then nodded before turning and moving deeper into the interior, his left knee buckling with each step.

It was one of those cramped little neighborhood hardware stores, merchandise stacked floor to ceiling, box fans and window sealant, key rings and copper wire, caulk, paintbrushes, batteries and screws, all in a tangle of passageways, like a nest. From the store's crowded center you couldn't see the windows, and it came to feel like the street was above, and you were way down in a hole where all that hardware had fallen.

We made turn after turn until the shelves finally broke to reveal the register. The man behind the counter looked up from his phone, bags under his eyes. Along the wall, packaged things hung on silver hooks. The boy touched them one by one, inquisitively, making a faint hum of deliberation in his throat.

"Anthony," the man at the register said and sighed. "Anthony. What're you looking for?"

The boy turned. When he spoke, he stuttered: "*Mousetraps.*"

"Anthony," said the man, shaking his head, pointing, "they're right in front of you."

The boy looked at the wall, then back at the man.

"Anthony," he said. "They're right in front of your face. They're right there." His pointed finger hung in the air. "In front of your face. Anthony, Jesus Christ." He groaned, pushed himself up, walked around the counter and over to us, reached to a spot on the wall behind me that neither the boy nor I had noticed: dozens of mousetraps.

"Mousetraps," the man said. "We got the Victor. And the Cat's Eye. Some people like those a little better. Easier to reuse, harder to catch a finger. But with the Victor if you don't mind you throw the whole thing out. *With* the mouse, I mean. They're less than a dollar apiece. How bad's the infestation?"

"Well," I said, "I've just seen the one. He's little. Like, a baby. I was thinking—do you have anything that might not kill the mouse?"

Then he looked me up and down, as if somehow he'd just noticed me for the first time.

He wrinkled his brow. "Not kill?" he asked.

"Like a humane trap, or—what do they call them, a catch and release?"

"Catch and release," he said, and grinned at the boy. "Like a fisherman, Anthony."

I looked over my shoulder, wishing for a glimpse of the street. The way he studied me, I felt naked, somehow, insufficient, like we all understood but couldn't say that I should have known not to come here, into this world of men and tools, hard measurements, the unbending laws of real things. I wished I'd dressed differently; I wished I'd worn different shoes.

He said, "You want humane traps?"

"Do you have them?"

"You want to set the mouse loose—where, in the park? At the playground?"

"Probably not the playground. I don't know, I hadn't thought about it. Do they work, the humane traps? Do you stock them?" I turned to search the wall.

He looked at the boy, then at me, shrugging apologetically. "For those, I'd have to go into the back." Now he spoke carefully. He seemed to have come to some judgment. There was a new ease in his body, a new subtlety to his speech. "Why don't you come with me?"

"Into the back?"

"Yeah," he said. "Right here. Anthony, show him."

The boy shuffled down the aisle to the right of the register, turned, and was out of sight.

"Back there?" I said.

"Yeah, of course, back there." He pointed.

Halfway down the aisle I turned to face him again. I gestured in the direction I'd seen the boy go. *There?* He nodded. When I reached the end of the aisle, at the store's back wall, I turned and saw Anthony, standing with ankles crossed, holding open a door. The small space on the other side was dimly lit. I could hear the man's unhurried footsteps approaching from behind.

"This is where the mousetraps are?" I called back.

He rounded the corner and pointed again. "This is the owner's office."

I had to duck to enter, and, once my eyes adjusted, I saw an elderly man in an ancient swivel chair behind a desk on which sat a nineteen-inch television. I hadn't seen one like it in years; I didn't know you could still use one, even. *The People's Court* was on.

He looked up at me, brows arched, then shot his eyes at Anthony.

"Louis said," Anthony explained, once he'd freed the *Lou* from his mouth.

Suddenly the man from behind the counter—Louis, I guessed—was behind me, close enough that I could feel his breath on my neck when he spoke. "Pop," he said. "This gentleman was inquiring after mousetraps. Humane mousetraps. The kind that don't kill."

The elderly man nodded, then pushed to half stand. He wore a white oxford shirt, unbuttoned at the top to reveal a spotted chest, and suspenders. "Take a seat. Let me turn off this noise." Reaching for the television's switch, he maintained something of his seated posture. "I'm Mr. Rugolo," he said.

"It's nice to meet you," I said.

He said, "Mousetraps."

"Yes." I swallowed. "I'd like to buy some."

"Let's talk first, just a little. You have mice?"

"Just one. That I've seen."

He considered it, working his jaw. "How do you know it's the same one?"

"Well, I guess I don't. But I think it is. He's little. A baby."

"Always," he said, "there are more than one. You see one, but there is more than one."

I told him I understood.

"And you don't want to kill the mouse. You want a special kind of trap. You want to release it, where, in the park? At the playground?"

"I asked the same thing, Pop," said Louis, suddenly jocular. "Didn't I—? Hey, what's your name, anyhow?"

"Of course," said Rugolo. "How rude."

"My name's Jeremy," I said. And because they watched expectantly, I added, "Booth. Jeremy Booth."

Anthony reentered with two paper cups full of coffee and set one before me, one before Rugolo.

"Please." Rugolo took up his cup delicately in both hands.

"Oh—that's okay. I'm not very thirsty."

"I insist."

Watery and sharp, the coffee made a strange perfume of the air below my nose.

"Very good." I nodded. "Thank you very much."

Rugolo said, "Are you scared of mice?"

The second sip caught in my throat; I coughed into my elbow. "Scared?"

He peered at me over his coffee, lips poised at the steaming rim.

I looked again over my shoulder; Louis watched me intently. "Well, no, I'm not, but . . ." Suddenly I felt the need to defend myself. "It's simply a question of hygiene. I won't have them in my apartment. I don't think that's unreasonable."

"Yes, yes, of course," said Rugolo. "Though it's not your apartment, strictly speaking. You rent, a young man like you?" He shrugged. "And some might say it's the building itself that invites the mice—its cracks and fissures, the imperfections that make, together, a record of the building's life. Do you know when your building was constructed, Jeremy Booth?"

The smile in his voice made my name sound like a child's. "Not—no, not precisely. It's a brownstone. Aren't they all from the—aren't they, like, nineteenth century?"

"The nineteenth century," he repeated, and smiled at Louis. "And you moved to the city when?"

"In 2013." I knew that was right, though under his gaze in that humid little room it was hard to focus; I felt some-how unsure.

"We've been in business fifty-eight years. My father opened this shop. And this is my son, this is Louis." He nodded at him.

I looked back at Anthony, standing in the doorway. "And your grandson?"

"No," said Rugolo, sadly. Then he put down his cup. "Jeremy Booth, if you aren't afraid of the mouse, why don't you want to kill it?"

Something in the question shocked me. "Well," I said, but found myself unable to go on.

Rugolo stared directly into my eyes.

"I just don't want to hurt the mouse—I don't want to hurt anything, really. The mouse hasn't done anything wrong. I don't know, it's what seems right to me. It's what seems natural."

Rugolo nodded gravely.

My answer had embarrassed me; I took a long sip of coffee. Then it struck me, the ridiculousness of the whole situation. "Pardon me," I said, "but do you have humane mousetraps to sell me or not?"

"I find it's a harder question than that," he said. "Because I want to warn you, Jeremy Booth, about the humane traps—you must check them regularly. They may not kill the mouse, but all the same they frighten him. You understand? The mouse will breathe very fast in the trap, his heart rate will accelerate, like this." He thumped himself rapidly with a stiff open hand. "He will urinate and defecate. If you do not check a so-called humane trap, it will kill the mouse just as surely as any wire trap. Secondly, if you catch a mouse and set it free too close, it will just run right back into the building. Mice live in groups. They're social creatures. They have families. They have children, Jeremy. The mouse will run right back into the building, and if he can't, if he cannot find a way, he will only keep trying, over and over, ceaselessly—his life will become a torture, a psychic torture. So. You must take the mouse away. One mile at least." He held up his index finger. "You should walk with the captured mouse deep into the park—out to the far side, where the Jamaicans live, okay?—and set the mouse free there. But you got to go quick, or the mouse might suffocate as you walk. And of course," he said, "after all your efforts, this too could mean death for the mouse, to be in a strange place so far from where he started. Is it better to kill the mouse all at once, with a snap?" He clapped his hands, then shrugged his shoulders.

I was beginning to feel very strange. The coffee had nauseated me; everything was too close; I could hear the breath whistling in Louis's nose. The room felt like it was moving. I squirmed in my seat, trying to blink the sensation away.

Rugolo stared into the dead TV screen, deep in thought. "People set mousetraps with cheese or peanut butter," he said, "but do you know what works better? String. Why? Because mice need small soft things, like bits of string, to build their nests. To build homes for their children. How long have you been living here, Jeremy? When did you move to the city?"

I couldn't think; I shook my head. "I don't know exactly."

Rugolo looked up at Louis, then reached for his coffee. "And you're not—if you don't mind me asking—you're not at work today. This is a weekday."

"I work freelance. I'm—I write copy. Advertising copy."

"An adman," he said, and grinned. "You didn't do the Super Bowl one, did you? The baby, the baby with the—with the—Louis, you know which one I mean?"

"The baby with the top hat," Louis said.

"The baby with the top hat. Did you write that one? We laughed and laughed."

"No," I said, removing my glasses, pinching the bridge of my nose. I was near to being sick.

"Jeremy, I want to tell you: I had a mouse once, in the bathroom. I set traps. Victor. Well, this mouse, after several days of successfully evading them, jumped somehow into the bucket of cleaning supplies we keep beside the toilet. And he couldn't get out." He curled his lips, shook his head. "Couldn't get out. I removed the cleaning supplies and with the bucket I walked outside. I watched him, as I went down the street, cowering there. His tail was all tensed, like this." He made a gesture with his hands, like closing them tight around a length of rope. "The bucket swung as I walked, Jeremy. I gave it no thought. But the mouse was intelligent enough, or clever enough—the word you might like to describe the mouse's mind, his thinking, I don't know—but the mouse was capable, you see, of apprehending that at the end of the bucket's backward arc, the angle was favorable to his jumping. And so, before I was able to get to the park, he did. He jumped. Outside he didn't look so big. I watched him, there on the sidewalk. Nighttime. Bitter cold. And in his face I saw something like bewilderment. I would have expected him to dash straight off and be gone. An escape worthy of an animal, you understand? Rushing, rushing, the thoughtless speed of instinct. But he only looked around—left, right—trying to understand what had happened. I don't know how their lives are, the mice. Possibly he'd never been outside, once, ever. Perhaps they live many generations without seeing the street." He sighed. "The mouse took several uncertain steps toward a pile of dead leaves. He nosed them cautiously. He slunk off the curb, nestled under the back tire of a parked car. He stood up, put his two little front paws on the tire. He was in a state of amazement."

Rugolo's face seemed too big, somehow. His whole head did. The room was getting darker. Strange mirages bred at the corners of my vision.

"So it's not easy," Rugolo said, "about the traps. Some might say the question is not so much about the traps themselves, or the mice, but about you. What kind of man you are." He leaned back, crossed his legs. "So?"

I shook my head. "What?"

"What kind of man are you, Jeremy?"

"I don't know."

"You don't know?"

I shook my head again, eyes closed, saliva pooling in my mouth.

He slapped his hand hard on the desk. "Are you unable to kill the object of your terror? Then what? What do you believe, Jeremy? Don't you know? How can you not know? Help me to understand."

When I stood, the room pitched. There were two doorways. From which had I entered? My legs buckled; I knocked into the table and sent my coffee onto the floor. "Oh God," I said, "I'm so sorry." But I knew if I bent down I'd be unable to stand back up. "Anthony can clean it," I offered. I didn't know why no one spoke; I looked from face to face.

Then I lurched toward the exit. The hall beyond it was dark and narrow. It didn't feel right, but I thought maybe it had become night, somehow, and the store was closed, all the lights off, and soon I'd see the glow of the street. Behind me were footsteps: Louis, following at a distance.

"Louis," I turned and shouted.

He walked slowly, head bowed as if in thought, hands in his pockets.

I pitched ahead. It was too dark to see, I rubbed my eyes and slapped at my face. But then, out ahead, I saw something. "It's sunlight!" I called back, triumphant. The path warmed with light, and then I was walking in mud, pungent, thick with mosquitoes. I pulled myself along on branches and vines, it was hot, summertime, deep and ripe. "Louis," I called. "Louis, you see? I'm nearly there!"

The trees grew greener, louder, birds and cicadas. Mud covered me to my knees. Louis walked beside me now, and below us was some little tributary, a road running above the embankment on its far side. I heard a car and turned to watch it pass—a blue station wagon.

"Can they see me, Louis?" Branches and leaves struck my face; thorns caught my trousers.

"They can see you."

"And they'll stop?"

"They may. Keep walking."

By dusk we were in a wide, green cornfield, early stars overhead. Beyond it, I saw headlights on a long highway. "Louis," I said. "I need to rest. Just a little while." I sank to the ground, chest heaving, eyes closed. "All right, Louis?"

But Louis was gone.

Winds cut the field; cars sang down the highway.

I'll go for help, I thought. I'll stand in the road, waving my hands.

"Louis, come back," I called.

In the distance, gas prices glowed over the prairie. A truck plaza. That's where I'd go. I walked to the edge of the highway, waited for a lull in the traffic, and ran across. The water in the bottom of my shoes was frigid now. There was a Love's, cars coming and going from the pumps. And beyond it, set back from the road, was a Cracker Barrel. I walked that way.

The hostess said they were closing soon but she would seat me. I'd never been in a Cracker Barrel before. Rock candy, board games, Christmas ornaments, all for sale in the gift shop there. She led me to a table in the dining room, placed a paper menu on it, and told me that my server would be right with me. I nodded. I ordered the pot roast. My mother used to make a pot roast. For my sides, I chose mashed potatoes and gravy, chicken dumplings, stewed green beans, and a broccoli casserole. And when the food came I devoured it. Heaped mashed potatoes onto the meat with my knife, ran a biscuit around the plate to mop the gravy. The waiter asked about dessert. I told him to leave the menu.

I supposed I would start by finding a room. I needed a shower. Then in the morning I could see about a change of clothes. Look for a ride. Ask about work.

The waiter came back. I wanted to know about the apple dumpling, which the menu described as "for two" and listed at 3,259 calories. I couldn't believe it—I asked how that could be right.

I would get back on my feet. Take my time. When I heard of something better, I'd move on to the next town. If I met the right person, I could even start a family. Raise some kids. Put away what I could. Be a good father, be nice to people. Stop to give directions. Leave a dollar in the tip jar. Weekends, holidays. Honest and simple. A new life. I would start that moment.

And more or less that's what I did.

# RETURN TO CRASHAW

ook. Up ahead, on the hillside, there are javelinas. Pec-caries, they're also called. One snub-nosed male and a few bristly females, nosing the soil. Two light-furred little ones underfoot. Tap the brakes, cut the wheel. Bring Jeep Nine to rest at the highway's dusty edge. Not too close, or the javelinas will scare. And now, though it is late in the day, summon what's left of your energy. Turn to your passengers. Say, "Would you forgive a brief interruption? Because we've got some wild pigs up on the hill there." Point. The hills are bare, ash brown, brutally unsheltered, though the sun's low, the warmth now bleeding from the rocks. "Indigenous to the region. They are adorable, folks, but only from a distance."

Someone cracks a window, and then there's a breeze.

Jeep Nine—a modified six-door nine-seater, pastel

blue, with the Crashaw Site logo stenciled in orange across the hood—smells of sunblock and bug spray, deodorized vinyl, musty vents.

Joe Blow leans up from the third row and says, "This isn't a wildlife tour. No one cares about pigs."

Don't let him rattle you. The binoculars are in the center console. Remove them, hold them to your eyes. Pull the focus until the javelinas are vivid and say, "Mr. Blow, that's ten additional points deducted for negativity." Then, in a show of goodwill, send the binoculars back over your shoulder to him. "It's Monday in America. Nothing's better than that."

Blow says, "Who cares about the pigs? Come on, let's go."

But Benjamin, seated beside you up front, says, "I'd like to look, Mr. Rose."

Thanks, Benjamin. He's ten or eleven, a Crashaw Foundation kid—applied with an essay and was awarded the travel package, airfare and a motel in Cascade, the little tourist hub, not unlike Keystone, South Dakota, or other gateway towns. The applications have reached an all-time low, supposedly, but Benjamin's so earnest and polite. You imagine he'd have won it in any era. He presses the binoculars to the lenses of his bright-red plastic glasses. Beside him is his fretful, enormous mother. What was her name? Resolve, again, to do better with the names. Outside the Visitor's Center, three times daily, you circle them up, introduce yourself, ask them to go around, and then—what? They tell you; you nod and smile, but you're someplace else. And is it worse this season than last? Worse now, in January, than December? In June, you'll be seventy-four. You've lived an absent-minded life, always one to misplace house keys, wallets, wristwatches. But lost or neglected things have this new way of startling you. Like sudden wonders, they'll appear: a blinker, flashing needlessly, or a blue flame left singing on the range.

Ask, "Shall we keep on?"

"I don't know," says Joe Blow, jittery and mean. "We could sit some more on the side of the road. You might tell us about the soil composition. Or the barometric pressure."

Deep breath. Put it into drive, step on the gas, still fussing with your seatbelt, which won't pull tight. Jeep Nine, the last of the old fleet, has been softened and worn by a long flow of strangers from around the world, packed three to a bench, shifting and stifling coughs. It's rugged and dented and tired. You have a soft spot for Nine, as for all well-loved, well-used things, but in Crashaw guide culture, Nine is bad luck. It's become a running joke. Last winter, Joy had road-sick triplets who vomited, simultaneously, in the second bench. The engine died on John Manyuru on the hottest day in August. And now here's Joe Blow, bearlike and sort of looming behind you, his Oakleys cutting a strip of outer space through the rearview. Never in your five seasons have you had such an asshole. Much less one with a firearm: When he climbed up into the Jeep, stooping and bending forward, you saw the imprint there on his waistband. At his four o'clock—a leftie. Well, these days, it's a fact of life. Since 2010 it's been legal on-site, everywhere but inside the Visitor's Center. Even so. Back in the parking lot, when you asked his name, he acted like he didn't hear. So you asked a second time. He was looking toward the horizon, one thick leg outside the circle. Clean-shaven white head, braided tattoos up his arms. "My name?" he repeated, and you said, Yes, sir, if you would. He thought a moment. Then he said, "You can call me Joe Blow."

At least there's Benjamin. Look at him, flipping through his *Little Illustrated Wonders Guide to the Crashaw Site*, matching the ruddy landscapes in his lap to the more vivid ones flying by outside—oceanic expanses studded with agave and mesquite.

And now here's Eileen, her voice, through the portable radio, in its dock up on the dash. Eileen's six years your junior; she's just returned for her second winter at Crashaw. You'd been anticipating her arrival—by the end of last March, you two were good friends. Today she's in Jeep Twelve, and you'd been hoping she'd run behind schedule, that your paths might overlap at the Scale Replica. Your groups would mill around then, taking pictures, and you and she could pair off, talking in that charmed, secret way two people have when they'd hoped to be brought together and then it happens. For the last few miles, an abstract version of that conversation has been playing out at the periphery of your awareness—not the lines, exactly, but the blocking, the feeling.

Rich, in the second row, leans forward and asks about

security. He's surprised there's not more. Rich is dressed badly for the desert in a linen blazer and glossy jeans. Apparently, he's some big-time artist. All the Crashaw artists-in-residence people were abuzz. Shael showed you Rich's stuff on his phone: ceramic sculptures of, for example, a Costco, or a Taco Bell, all covered in ivy. Beside Rich is Mustache: dark-skinned, with a bald head and fedora and safari shirt. All afternoon, the two of them have been engaged in some inscrutable whispered argument.

Tell Rich that, in truth, there's not much of anything out here. The Crashaw Site was demilitarized in 1986. The era of barbed wire and army trucks is long past. Now it's administered by the Bureau of Land Management. Consider that, from Cascade, it's a ten-mile shuttle ride to the gates on a lonely highway, all desert, undeveloped, then two miles more to the Visitor's Center, and beyond that, another twelve to the Site itself.

Rich says he knows all that; it's not his first trip to Crashaw. "What I mean is I'm surprised there's not more security *now*—after last summer."

Of course. In July, two people, a man and a woman, hiked up the mountains in the dark, crossed the perimeter illegally, entered the Site, climbed the Needle—the Site's tallest megalith, nicknamed for its resemblance to a giant stone sewing needle, rising steadily from the earth at a roughly ten-degree angle—and jumped. From the highest point, right down through the Eye. About a hundred feet. In the morning, a team in from France found the bodies on the desert floor. They were young, drifting.

They'd spent the last several weeks of their lives with the Full Timers, a loose-knit group of Site worshippers who, for decades now, have kept up a rainbow tent city off the highway just outside the gates. For a few weeks, Crashaw was back in the news.

To Rich, say, "You know, I'm a snowbird. I wasn't here when that happened."

Turn left, onto Marathon.

"Yeah, but," says Rich, "isn't it a liability? Like, those tent people—what if they all rushed in together?"

Ben's mother asks could we please change the topic.

Absolutely. First, though, reassure Rich: "Did you get a look at the Full Timers on your way in? They're not the violent type. Nor are they so very well organized. I personally, just by the way, would not recommend the free meals they advertise on those billboards."

Mustache chuckles. This relaxes you by one or two degrees.

But Marianne, beside Rich on the second bench, asks why not. Maybe twenty, freckled and blond, dressed to hike in high-waisted green nylon shorts. You'd thought she was sleeping. "I was there. The people, they are kind. They eat only vegetarian. For us it was good." Marianne's Quebecois. At the Visitor's Center, you heard her telling Mustache that she'd spent the summer picking cherries, made some friends that way, and together they'd skipped the fall semester to travel down through the States. She was the only one among them who'd wanted or been able to pay the ninety dollars for the tour—which is exactly what that price point is designed to accomplish. There remains a vocal crowd among the academics who think the public shouldn't be allowed anywhere near the Crashaw Site. Not while so little is yet understood about it.

Tell Marianne you didn't mean much by that and you're glad she enjoyed it. When you try to catch her eye in the mirror, she's leaned back again, eyes closed. Which strikes you as odd.

But now Mom of Ben is on edge. She says, "So, it's all a bunch of nuts that come out here?"

Benjamin, without shifting his gaze, takes hold of her hand.

You can concede to her that, yes, Crashaw does attract passionate types. This is diplomatic wording. Evenings, in Eulalia—across the federal land from Cascade, where the guides, artists in residence, academics, archaeologists, and anyone else out for a season rent rooms or sagging houses or scattered trailers—people gather on the porch of the Way Station, the little tavern. With bottles of beer, they sit on mismatched folding chairs, sing cowboy songs, talk about Crashaw and the desert and life back home. And when the guides swap stories about the day's tourists, it's with particular emphasis on the nuts: religious freaks, Crashaw cultists, UFO types, orb spotters, New Agers, spellcasters, psychonauts. Just last week, Kim had a family of seven, bright blond, all in matching formalwear, that spoke in tongues and rolled like snakes up on the East Observation Tower. As a matter of fact, that was in Jeep Nine.

Tell Ben's mom, "We get our share of oddballs. So does Stonehenge. So does the White House."

Then Joe Blow says, "Hey."

Look up at the mirror.

"Your turn signal's on."

Sudden wonders. The arrow blinks toward nothing but the hills.

Reach to flick it off. And tell Joe Blow it's a good thing he's paying such close attention.

Turn onto Grapevine, a dirt road, the intersection unmarked, and drive through prickly pear, tufts of dry grass, striated rock in little towers. The Scale Replica is two miles ahead. And look, here's Jeep Twelve, traveling in the opposite direction. So Eileen didn't run late after all. She beeps twice, grinning, her hair radiantly white through the windshield. Then you clatter past each other. It was about this time last year that you and Eileen fell in together, drinking coffee first thing in the mornings, driving out through the desert or into Cascade on days off. Since your wife, Joan, passed away, you've lived alone, and certain habits come back easily; they want to come back. It's good to meet someone's eyes in moments of subtle amusement, to catalogue things to tell that person at day's end. After the season, you called Eileen a few times at her house in Iowa City. But then, once, her husband picked up. She'd never talked much about him, other than to confide, across a few quiet evenings, how unhappy they'd long been. It startled you to hear him say hello—in an amiably detached tone of voice, like the phone were near a window and the summer was beautiful.

The Replica is built at 30 percent scale. It has a tendency to underwhelm: Visitors often say the actual structures look smaller, in real life, than they'd expected. But consider what Jeremiah Wolfe, Crashaw's educational director, says about the Scale Replica: that Crashaw isn't something you can just drop into the people's laps. Before observing the genuine megaliths, they'll need conceptual scaffolding, something solid to touch, stand under, walk through. Properly engaged, the Replica serves as a multidimensional primer: on the sudden materialization, discovery, and excavation of the structures; early-days attempts at debunking the Site as a hoax; government seizure of the Crashaw family's ranch land; various academic, philosophical, religious, and moral responses, including attempts to communicate with the structures, determine their status as a potential threat or incursion, and to substantiate claims that the Site exerts an effect on consciousness for those in close proximity.

This is all true. But you like the Replica because it's good for kids.

Coast down the hill, preparing to deliver your remarks, as well-worn and comfortable to you as this stretch of road. Look at the Needle. The way it dominates, visually, with the Shark's Teeth, the Light Bulbs, and the Reef—more nicknames, bestowed for obvious reasons—scattered around it, as if in orbit. It's natural to perceive the Needle as central. But then, we have no understanding of Crashaw's origins or purpose. We are looking with human eyes. At what, we don't know.

"Let's skip this," says Joe Blow. "It's stupid. Let's skip it."

"Actually, I'm with Joe Blow," says Rick. *Rick*—not Rich. It's Rick. "Must we?"

"Don't be rude," Mustache says. "Ignore him, Mr. Rose. You're doing great."

Point through the windshield. "Benjamin. Look at the Needle there. You know, to me, it's always looked more like an upside-down hockey stick. Because of the Eye—the way the Eye levels off and runs parallel to the ground. In August 1972, Jerry Crashaw rode up onto the ridge, looked down into the valley, and saw it there—the Needle, half buried, and the smaller structures around it, presenting just then as a series of mounds—"

"This is fake," Blow says. "Just take us to the real thing. Take us to the Observation Towers."

"I'm sorry," Mustache says, "but would you let him talk?"

You're failing. You've lost them. A pang of sadness.

Ask Benjamin where you were.

Benjamin: "A series of mounds."

"Good. So it wasn't until excavation began that we understood the scale of the Site—the Eye, more than thirty meters up from the base of the Needle; the Light Bulbs, five meters high each; and the Shark's Teeth, two meters. And second, the Reef was uncovered. The Reef is particularly interesting, because none of the other structures bear markings of any kind. With the exception of—"

"The raised lines in Light Bulb Three," says Benjamin, seatbelt off his shoulder and knees on the seat, looking out the window like a puppy.

"But," says Rick, "we know all this. Anyway, you're talking about it as if *these* are the real structures, and that's . . ." He sighs. "Deeply problematic." Rick says he's sorry, it's not your fault, he knows you're just doing your job. But the public shouldn't be forced to engage with the Scale Replica, which helps to suggest, quite falsely, that the mystery of the Crashaw Site is somehow *containable*. The Replica deliberately obscures and confounds the Site's spiritual aspects in anodyne bullshit about the structures' dimensions—how tall and how wide. It diminishes the subsequent experience on the Observation Towers. Really, it's borderline criminal.

Mustache says, "He's like this all the time."

"But he's right," says Joe Blow. "We don't want to stop here. Let's keep going."

Tell them that there are a couple of things, interesting things, you want to point out.

"Why don't we put it to a vote," Blow says.

Tell him there's no vote.

"Raise your hand," Blow says, "if you want to stop here."

A wave of despair. It feels like they could do it, like you really might be voted out.

But up goes Benjamin's hand. And, actually, that appears to settle it.

Twenty minutes. Take a breather in the shade of Light Bulb Three—the Replica's version, with the wayside exhibit on the failure of conventional approaches to Crashaw. The Site presents as a group of large sandstone monuments; we can agree on that. But we don't know how to study it. The initial impulse was to treat it as an archaeological dig, though having appeared so abruptly, the structures are devoid of context. Stratigraphy and relative dating are useless. We've found no remnants of tools, or any correspondences, stylistic or otherwise, to the work of known megalith builders. But neither, really, did anyone expect to find such things—nor is there widespread agreement as to the appropriateness of terms like *builders* or *built*.

What a shitty group. It's okay to think it.

Joe Blow. He's what Joan would have called a bad actor. Look at him, walking there, so loathsome as he reaches to scratch the deep middle of his back. Big but soft—thirty years ago, you're fairly sure, you could have taken him. Not now. The truth is that you're vulnerable, driving strangers into the desert every day. It all hinges on them being good people. Joe Blow could be some sort of malcontent, or extremist. These things do happen. A conspiracy theorist who believes there are tunnels under the Site, or that it's a hologram. And the quiet here is almost eerie: the day's last group, no others behind you. You could radio security. Chalk it up to an abundance of caution. But then, wouldn't that be a little hysterical? You'd hate to give the impression that you can't manage.

Anyway, complaints about the Replica are nothing new. Place one hand flat to Light Bulb Three, the Replica's version, against those raised lines. Note the theme-park quality of the fake rock. The Replica was built in the early 2000s, and it feels dated to that era—the design of the waysides, the color-coded walking paths. On New Year's Eve, everyone in Eulalia goes to the Site at sundown. Not to the Observation Towers. Down to the Site itself. An exception is made; it's tradition. The desert's cool, the sky is holy. One star appears, then another. Sometimes you start to walk with someone, out through the Light Bulbs, speaking in whispers, and then after a while you notice you're alone. You hear the wind overhead and it sounds like something else. The questions you have about Crashaw become questions about yourself. You forget your body, let it mill about while your mind just floats. The first time you stood underneath the Needle, you knew the moment would stay in you. And it did. You looked up. The Eye was like a picture frame. You watched the stars.

Back into Nine, one by one, seatbelts buckled, brows wiped, water bottles uncapped and sipped.

"Very good," you say and throw it into reverse.

Joe Blow says, "What about Marianne?"

In the rearview, her seatbelt lies unbuckled across the canvas seat.

Shift back into park. Say, "Of course. Marianne. Any-one seen Marianne?"

Blow shakes his head, disgusted.

No sign of her. Ask did anyone learn anything in-teresting.

Mustache, God bless him, talks at length about the wayside exhibit concerning modern holistic movements in Crashaw studies. Some argue that what we *can* study effectively, if not the basic facts of the Site's origins, is its outbranching network of cultural effects—the work that its presence performs in our world. What, in other words, has changed since the structures appeared? They're look-ing systematically now at depictions of the Crashaw Site in media, various political and religious responses, and ultimately, measurable shifts in attitude that might be correlated to the propagation of information regard-ing the Site. At the fringe of that field is the idea that Crashaw may be best understood as a kind of sustained apparition—paradoxical, poetic, mythic—whose physi-cality isn't entirely the point.

Respond with vague affirmations, beeping the horn now and then. All's still through the windshield, no flash of that green nylon. From the radio comes a small burst of static. Don't call this in yet; it'd just mean trouble for you. You've never heard of a guide losing a visitor. Give it three more minutes. Mom of Ben scrolls fruitlessly on her phone, a downtime habit that visitors can't kick, you've noticed, despite the total lack of signal anywhere between here and Cascade. Mustache and Rick argue over whether or not the Replica is camp. Imagine sinking through the driver's seat into some calmer, bluer world. Where would that be? Yesterday. Near twilight, on the Way Station's porch. The whole crowd's out. The sky's a royal shade. Take the open folding chair next to Eileen's. She touches your arm. Turquoise bangles on her wrist.

Rick says, "There she is."

Turn. Marianne's way up on the hillside behind the Replica. Draw a breath. Unbuckle your seatbelt. Take the radio from the dock. Before you go, ask Benjamin why you can't starve in the desert.

He looks up through those absurd red glasses.

Smile. Tell him it's because of all the sand which is there.

Take the hill in big strides, pushing your hands into your thighs as you ascend. Your warming muscles carry the memories of a lifetime spent out of doors. Boyhood in Clackamas County, Oregon, down in the woods with brother Doug, whacking nettles and hogweed with big sticks, lifting broad stones with both hands to drop into the creek. Then mountain climbing in leather boots and wool socks, bandaging your blisters at night in the hut. Moths flown into the tent in August. Autumn mornings, instant coffee. With Joan, after you were married, climbing Steens Mountain. Then carrying Sam up the trails on your back when he was a baby. And Christine four years later. Those hills wetter and greener than these. Birds in formation overhead. Everyone must reach a point of perfect articulation. This is a pet theory that's been years in the distant reaches of your mind. Some point of completion at which you are finally and authentically yourself, for better or worse, and everything that leads to that time is an approach, and all that follows a recession. For you, it must have been in the long-past years that you spent in communion with other bodies, Joan's and Sam's and Christine's. It must have been in the way you lived then, with the warmth and weight of other arms and legs and hind quarters pressing on you, pulling you down, little heads resting or crying or pouting on your shoulder. You get used to bearing that weight.

Marianne sits cross-legged, her back to you. Walk around to face her, lower yourself down onto the dust there. Don't worry that it takes a while. Get comfortable. You want this to go well. The radio digs into your side; unclip it from your belt and set it down. Pull up your left knee, then your right, wrap your arms around them. In conversation, you should look people directly in the eyes. This is an important bit of wisdom. Marianne's gaze is turned skyward, her face lined and almost hardened, despite her youth, from sun and wind. Behind her, down the hill, is the Scale Replica, and Jeep Nine, its blue so piercing against the landscape.

"The air," Marianne says and inhales deeply.

On the drug thing, you're of a see-no-evil mindset. It's not that you're so sympathetic to drug use. Not once in your life have you consumed an illicit substance. That's no point of pride; it's just how things were, when and where you came up. But here, the official policy—in place as a deterrent, the problem being so pervasive—is to radio any drug use in at once and turn the tour around. That's an undue pressure on the guides, for one. You're not the police. And second, the stoned people are if anything less trouble than the average tourist. They keep to themselves. In practice, it's almost always best to let it slide.

Tell her, "Marianne, if you took something, that's fine. The thing is, I just don't want to know about it."

Marianne says, "I took LSD and Molly."

Nod. Pick up a flat stone with your left hand. Turn it over, wondering, as often you do, how Joan would have handled it. The best they could do is get on standby for tomorrow. They traveled to be here; they rented rooms. Poor Benjamin, with his prizewinning essay. What if he flies home in the morning?

Marianne reaches out, takes the stone from you, gazes into it.

Put your weight back onto your hands, begin to push up. Ask Marianne if she's safe and comfortable. Ask if she's thirsty, and whether she can keep a secret. Remind her, as you stand, that it's Monday in America.

When Rick asks, tell him of course she's okay, why wouldn't she be okay? Marianne climbs up into her seat, and Rick clarifies that he wants to know if she's too high, should we be concerned, does she need some kind of health check? Mustache tells him to be quiet. But Mom of Benjamin, physically repelled, squirming back into the window and putting both arms around her son, says, "She's *high*?" Protest that no, Marianne's not high. "Yes I am," pipes Marianne. Rub both eyes with your hands. "High on *drugs*?" gasps Mom of Ben. Now everyone's talking at once. "He has to take us back," says Rick, exasperated. "We all got the same lecture at the Visitor's Center." Joe Blow says he's not going back—he came all this way to see the Site and that's what he's going to do. Mom of Ben wants to know what happens if her son gets a contact high. What if you *all* get a contact high? Rick says this is your fault, that you're in charge, you should have been paying attention, and Mustache tells him to quit being so severe all the time, it's exhausting. Blow repeats about not going back, so calm and assured that it's hard not to see it as a threat. Is it a threat? Because what's he mean, that he'd put up some kind of fight? That he'd menace or bully or harm you? Is he referring to the gun in his waistband? Watching him sulk there in the rearview you want to kill him, the urge is real— you want to lunge at Joe Blow, tear off the sunglasses, and press into his eyes until they burst. Mom of Ben asks what happens if Marianne snaps and starts to think she's a glass of orange juice, or that she can fly. Marianne says, "Hey, I'm right here—you can just, like, talk to me."

Say, "Okay, listen."

And when they keep arguing, shout it. Surprise yourself, finding a voice you haven't used in years. *Okay. Listen.* Now they're quiet. Say, "Here's what's going to happen. Yes, Marianne is on drugs. It's not ideal. Benjamin, don't be scared. She's still a good person. We have to go back. But. We'll go along Gap Road, via the North Observation Tower. We'll stop there briefly. You can see Crashaw. We will forgo the South Observation Tower and the East. I'm sorry for the disappointment. But that's the plan."

Benjamin's looking up at you, lips slightly parted.

Clear your throat. Say, "As long as that's all right by you, Ben."

Wait for his nod.


Well, how *would* it be—to walk up the Needle and fall through the Eye? Why would you do it? Because, afterward, everything would be quiet. Because it's hard to be alive in a body, no matter what. And all the best of your life is now so vanishingly remote as to feel alien. Sam lives in Los Angeles, Christine in Vancouver. December the tenth marked six years since Joan died. And if this isn't your last season at Crashaw, it will have to be the next, or the one after that, and then you'll be alone year-round in Oregon. And what then? Your father died just eight years older than you are now. In a nursing home, after breakfast, watching TV in a wheelchair. Having drifted into that wayward state. Mistaking you always for Donald, his brother, or Ed Metz, from the Navy, or Gabriel, a nurse who'd once worked there. Why should you be any different? It's happening now. You'll drift, as if through space, past the threshold of utility, then competence, then cognizance. Always less of use, less noticed and cared for. Until finally you're alone within yourself. How much longer? It could be six years, or eight. It could be ten years. It could be twelve.

The North Observation Tower is an open platform up six flights of corrugated metal steps. They've filed wordlessly out of Nine and started up. Sit sideways in the driver's seat, door open, feet in the dirt. It rankles, to think that you came here—violating protocol, inviting consequence—under pressure from Blow. But focus on Benjamin. And hope that the rest of them feel sufficiently placated to just leave without complaint. Aim to slip quietly back into the Visitor's Center. Drop them at the shuttle. You'll never see these people again.

Now step out of the Jeep and close the door. Climb the steps. Feel the breeze, that high current, near the top. The land runs so far in every direction, it's like looking out to sea. Across the platform, at the railing, the five of them stand in a line, backs to you. The wide shadow visible beyond them is the excavation. Like a crater, or caldera. Off to your left, in the distance, is the East Observation Tower. One of the dimly visible people descending its steps is Eileen. The late sun smolders in the west. Right here is where your old photo was taken. The four of you, just where they are now, though turned to face the camera. Sam in braces. Christine, then so attention starved, in that chorus-line pose. You and Joan together. Her hair cut short that year. Cross the platform. Put a hand up on the railing. Below you now is the Crashaw Site. Long shadows run eastward under the Shark's Teeth and Light Bulbs. The Needle points straight west into the sun. Despite everything, it is calm here. On an ordinary day, you might call it that last-tour feeling: the absence of other groups, all quiet down at the Site. But now it must be the structures themselves. They do exert a pull. Maybe your group feels it, too—look how it's hushed them. We're built the same, after all. The air is cool now, the light deeper. A red-tailed hawk circles slowly over the Site. Don't break this silence too soon. There's an art to it. Let the right moment come. Then you'll go home.

But, behind you, Joe Blow is already halfway down the platform's steps.

Mustache asks, "Where's he going? Can't we stay a little longer?"

And by the time you've crossed back to the far side to look over the railing, Blow is down on the ground, walking briskly past Nine and out toward Gap Road.

Be mindful of your left knee, which aches and wobbles down steps like these. The fact that the others stay close at your heels as you descend, peppering you with questions, makes you feel sullen and abused. You just need a minute to sort this out. On the staircase's east-facing flights, you can see Joe Blow, his bald head, red shirt, working legs. Facing west, the landscape is blank.

Now here's level ground. Trot past the Jeep, calling to him. He's hit Gap Road, thirty yards out, and turned south. Toward the Site. But there's nothing wild in him, no panic. As you close in, consider reaching out, grabbing his shirt collar or shoulder, or even trying for a headlock. Instead, fall in beside Joe Blow. Look at his face. Under the sunglasses, he may be crying. His shoulders have fallen, causing his belly to bulge. He moves like he's come out onto this road after wandering lost in the desert for hours.

Joe Blow says he has to be there with it. There's something he has to find out; he needs to know something. Tell him that's impossible—he has to turn back. He asks who says so. You? All through his long drive to Cascade, Blow couldn't shake the idea that he'd receive a sign. Something to show him, yes or no, what to do. So he watched closely, and look, this whole day has been one big arrow pointing him straight to the Site. It's humbling, astonishing—if you hadn't left the radio up on that hill with Marianne, who knows what might have happened?

Stop walking. Grope wildly about your waist.

In despair, now, you can see the radio, right where you set it down, on its side, in the dirt, five miles from here.

The rest of them have been keeping pace uncertainly a few yards back. Now they gather beside you as Blow walks on ahead. Mustache puts an arm around your shoulders, a gesture of consolation so unexpected that you're nearly overcome. "What do we do?" he asks. But your mouth is too dry to answer. By the time you've managed to go and alert anyone, Blow will be there, and he knows it. You're alone here in the desert, connected to nothing.

Permutations are outlined and considered, though it's hard to think, and your tongue's gone numb. When you go back over all this, filling in details, retelling it to yourself—

tomorrow before dawn, for example, in bed, half awake—
these moments will seem indistinct, like something you'd
observed from someplace else. You'll just have to go with
him. Since you can't prevent Joe Blow from entering the
Site, it's all you can do—accompany him, try to keep him
safe. But Rick protests: Not by yourself. He'll go with you.
And now Marianne, her pupils as big as dinner plates, says
she wants to go, too. Why don't you all go? "Because it's
trespassing," says Mustache, and Marianne considers that,
then says that if no one can report it, she doubts that's
true. Like if a tree falls in the forest. These people are your
responsibility, each one, and together. And now Mom of
Ben is in tears. She won't be left there on the roadside
with her son. Bitterly, in anger, she declares this the worst
trip of her entire life. You're sure that's true, and what's
more, this must be the worst tour in the history of the
Crashaw Site, and you the very worst guide.

The unpaved access road makes switchbacks up to a tight
place between two slabs of rock where it narrows almost
to nothing. On the far side, it descends sharply to Crashaw.
Joe Blow is at the wheel of Jeep Nine. That's the condition
he proposed, and you agreed, so long as he stowed the gun
and holster in the back. Now he lets the Jeep coast over
the incline and down to where the road levels out, then
ends. Like driving onto the Salt Flats. Breathe deep. The
sun's in your eyes, the structures out ahead, like some
unearthly city from this vantage.

Light Bulb Eight, the easternmost structure, is the first

that you pass. Everyone turns to watch it receding. Now here are the Shark's Teeth, outcroppings of the Reef, and beyond, the Needle.

Benjamin leans up from the third row and says, "Excuse me." Though timid, his voice startles you. You're unsure who he's addressing. Blow looks into the rearview. "Would it be possible," Benjamin asks, "to stop up here?" He points at Light Bulb Three.

The rules now are unclear. Maybe that's why Blow does it. Veers toward the Light Bulb, shifts into park at a respectful distance. Doors open. No one speaks above a whisper. Light Bulb Three, fifteen yards out, is beautiful at this hour. Benjamin sets down his backpack, takes out a *Crashaw Kids* notebook, holds it tight in both hands. He begins to move toward Light Bulb Three. When he reaches it, the structure looming over him, he turns around, looks at the group as if about to speak. Then he turns back, lays his right hand flat against the stone, and traces his fingers over the raised lines. There are five of them, running from the Light Bulb's base up to its pole. The lines are thin and tight to one another, like the inverse of what a small rake would leave in sand. Benjamin tears a blank page from the notebook, presses it to the rock, and makes a pencil etching of the lines. His movements are unhurried, face bent close to the page. When he's done, he slips the page back into the notebook. He looks straight up the Light Bulb's face. He returns, surprising you with an apologetic touch on the arm. Then he takes his mother by the hand and walks off with her, deeper into the Site.

The group disperses.

In the summer of 1960, eleven years old, you were crazy for Mars. With bedsheets hung over the windows, you'd pretend that your room was a rocket flying there. The darkness made it real. Afternoon light brightened the edges of the bedsheets, and everything within the room was shades of blue. Your focus was so complete that each time you tore down the sheets, the sight of your yard, the garage and driveway, felt wrong. You would press your forehead to the glass, feeling strange and solitary and far apart from something vital. Maybe that memory is so near at hand because this, here, now is what you felt you should have seen through your windows. The Martian landscape was redder, in your mind, and empty. No structures. But isn't the feeling the same? Maybe that summer you weren't consumed by fantasies of Mars at all but by this, this later place in your life—maybe time can move like that, on secret currents, and some part of this moment is traveling back to that other you, in his room, hanging bedsheets over the curtain rods.

Joe Blow is walking toward the Needle. Follow him. But keep your distance. He said there's something he needs to know. What did he mean? Off to your left are more javelinas. At rest on their sides. One raises its head to watch you. It works its jowls, watching, then lays its head back down. Mustache's name, by the way, is Terrence. He and Rick are out by Shark's Tooth Six, talking in whispers about Rick's father, who died last summer. Rick hadn't expected the feeling of failure that nagged at him afterward. A deeper way of being between the two of them feels possible only now that he's gone. Marianne walks through the Reef with her eyes closed. Benjamin and Josephine, his mother, stand looking at Light Bulb One. Hand in hand.

The first few steps up the Needle are nothing at all. The slope is gentle; the rock is wide. To Joe Blow, it looks like the broken mast of a wrecked ship. The Eye a crow's nest. When he glances back at you, keep your eyes low. Don't crowd him. And be careful. The rock is wide, yes, but rounded, like a column. Ten feet up, then fifteen. Move into a crouch. One motion, then another.

The rock is sun warmed but cooling. Grit clings to your palms. Your mind is empty and clear; there's no static now. Climb until the bushes and blue Jeep and the rounded tops of the Light Bulbs below have the too-perfect quality of miniatures. The wind is picking up. It's natural to be frightened. But lift your left hand, reach forward, place it down. You have to. Lift your right foot, pull it up, place it down. Joe Blow sees things and their shadows all at once. Out on the horizon, he sees a charcoaled place that must be a distant rainstorm. He can almost taste the stone, a mineral essence on his tongue, some effect of the air and dust and his own exertion. Just above him, the Eye juts out over the desert.

Behind you now, climbing the Needle, is Rick. Behind Rick is Terrence. Behind Terrence, if you can believe it, is Marianne. Calling out to one another about footing and smooth spots. There's more sky up here, deeper bands of color. With each movement, the Site drops farther away. Your legs are still strong, though slow to respond. Your hands slide when they shouldn't. But each new step is just work to be done. You've never been afraid of work. This is Monday in America.

Now, on all fours, Blow crawls onto the rim of the Eye. He takes it clockwise. Under his breath he's repeating the word *okay*. He lives differently than you did. You have never undertaken anything like the long trip he made here, two days and nights in the car, not a word to anyone, without even packing a bag. Way out in the middle, arms shaking, he comes into a seated position. Lets his left leg over the rim, then his right. And now he's sitting on the Eye. Feet dangling, for all the world like it were a swimming pool. Almond-shaped, a mandorla. Follow him. To understand rationally that the rim is plenty wide, that there's no way, really, the wind could buffet you off, is not the same as believing it. Your limbs are weak and trembling. But you're almost there. Just don't look down. This is an important bit of wisdom. Now come and sit beside him. Chest heaving. A long, exhausted sigh. Your feet unsupported beside his.

And here are the rest, crawling onto the rim, one by one. Split by sunlight, half shadowed.

Briefly, close your eyes.

Now that you're here, you don't quite know what you're meant to do. There's the North Observation Tower. Over there's the access road. That's the place, one hundred feet down, where you stood looking up that first night. There's no temptation to speak. Words would be graceless. But you'd give him something if you could. Time passes. You find yourself thinking about Joan. She moved to hospice care and came home. You pushed the bed up against the windows. The leaves changed, then came down. You sat with her, held her hand, sometimes lay down beside her. One afternoon, when she'd been silent and still for many hours, she swallowed, then began to move her mouth. You leaned close to hear. She said, "Walking." A croak, her lungs full of fluid. You pressed your forehead to her cheek. "You're walking?" you asked. She said, "Yeah." As if surprised. Her mouth was open. A long moment passed. You asked, "Where?"

The sun's now gone behind the ridge. The stars here are really something. At night you can see nebulas, the Milky Way, lights shooting across the sky. Great horned owls nest, from time to time, atop the Light Bulbs. They pick mice and small lizards from the creosote patches below and have been doing so for millions of years. It's getting cold now. Time to go home. Don't say so; he knows. Marianne's swinging her legs up onto the rim. And Rick, and Terrence. Crawling back toward that oblique column. He'll go next. Then you. Going down will be easier than coming up.

Eulalia was once a silver mining town. The old miners' graveyard sits on the south side of the state road. Piles of rocks mark some graves. Others have monuments in a

Mexican style: white stepped pyramids adorned with cala-veras and images of the Virgin.

It's dark out. On the Way Station's porch, Pete leads the little circle of pickers. Eileen sips from a bottle of beer. The folding chair next to hers is open. They're wonder-ing what's kept you. Someone says to take into account that you had Nine. Anything's liable to have happened. Number Nine, says someone else, dolefully. For a moment the conversation is general. Then Pete says he's got one. He strums some chords on his guitar. They hang in the air like a natural feature of the evening. The other play-ers pick up the changes. Pete's voice strains; he's maybe not in the best key. He reaches the chorus, and a handful of others join in. You don't know this song. From here, in the lot—outside the porch light's reach, where you've found yourself lingering—you can't quite make out the words. But it's the sound that matters. The singers' voices overlap; together they fill the space made by the light. Stay here, listening, just a while longer. Hands in your pockets against the chill. Head back, lips parted. The whole sky's porous with stars. No one knows the second verse, so Pete starts the first one again.

# ACKNOWLEDGMENTS

"The New Toe" borrows lines from Richard Scarry's *Cars and Trucks and Things That Go.*

The passage about Mars in "Return to Crashaw" is an allusion to *The Secret School* by Whitley Strieber, a writer whose work is dear to me.

I am boundlessly grateful to Claudia Ballard for her faith in, critical eye for, and expert stewardship of these stories. Thanks, too, to everyone at William Morris Endeavor, especially Fiona Baird and Laura Bonner. Thomas Gebremedhin, my editor, always saw straight to the heart of these stories—most critically, when I myself could not. He did so much to shape this book. My deepest thanks to him and to the rest of the team at Doubleday, especially Emily Mahon, Eddie Allen, Casey Hampton, Elena Hershey, Jess Deitcher, and Johanna

Zwirner. Thanks also to Hermione Thompson and everyone at Hamish Hamilton. And to Alexander Fest.

My deepest thanks to everyone who taught me about writing: Kevin Attell, Douglas Basford, Bill Bickley, Tristan Davies, Patricia Davis, Stephen Dixon, Jonathan Safran Foer, Jeri Johnson, Hari Kunzru, David Lipsky, Terry Maguire, Jean McGarry, Joyce Carol Oates, Julie Orringer, Darryl Pinckney, and Michael Wood, among many others. Particularly heartfelt thanks to Jeffrey Eugenides, Katie Kitamura, and Zadie Smith, all of whom were exceptionally generous and helpful with these stories both during my time at NYU and afterward.

I am profoundly grateful for the support of Stanford University and the Wallace Stegner Fellowship, without which I could not have completed this book. And to Adam Johnson, Chang-rae Lee, and Elizabeth Tallent, whose mentorship and instruction changed who I am as a writer. Thanks and love, too, to my Stegner cohort.

My thanks to Emily Stokes, Deborah Treisman, and James Yeh for editing several of these stories and vastly improving them in each case.

Heartfelt thanks to Douglas Watson for his reading, encouragement, and guidance. And to Patrick Doerksen, Molly Johnsen, and Brett Wisniewski, both for their help as early readers, and for all the hours of excited conversation, recommendation-trading, and idea-generating. Thanks, too, to Jim Canning, whose example meant a lot to me.

Above all, thank you to my parents, to Louise and Eliot, and most importantly, to Rosalie, Raymond, and Audrey.